ON THE EDGE

ESPECIALLY FOR GIRLS™
presents

ON THE EDGE

Written by
Kate William

Created by
FRANCINE PASCAL

BANTAM BOOKS
TORONTO · NEW YORK · LONDON · SYDNEY · AUCKLAND

This book is a presentation of **Especially for Girls**™ Weekly Reader Books.
Weekly Reader Books offers book clubs for children from preschool
through high school.
For further information write to:
Weekly Reader Books, 4343 Equity Drive, Columbus, Ohio 43228.

Published by arrangement with Bantam Books, a division
of Bantam Doubleday Dell Publishing Group, Inc.
All Rights Reserved.
Especially for Girls and Weekly Reader are trademarks of
Field Publications.
Printed in the United States of America.

ON THE EDGE

A Bantam Book / October 1987

Grateful acknowledgement is made for permission to reprint the poem
"Dirge Without Music" by Edna St. Vincent Millay. From *Collected Poems,*
Harper & Row. Copyright © 1928, 1955 by Edna St. Vincent Millay and
Norma Millay Ellis. Reprinted by permission.

Sweet Valley High is a registered trademark of Francine Pascal.

Conceived by Francine Pascal

Produced by Cloverdale Press, Inc.
133 Fifth Avenue, New York, NY 10003

Cover art by James Mathewuse

ISBN 0-553-26703-5

One

Jessica Wakefield flipped her sun-streaked blond hair back, and checked her appearance in the locker-room mirror with obvious satisfaction. She loved her cheerleading costume. The red cotton sweater really made her blue-green eyes stand out, and the white pleated skirt showed her long, tanned legs off to perfect advantage. Jessica loved cheerleading. She prided herself on being one of the most visible members of the junior class at Sweet Valley High, and she did everything possible to make sure that wherever the action was, she'd be right in the thick of it.

Her reverie was shattered as the door to the locker room burst open and the rest of the squad came hurrying in. "Jess!" Amy Sutton exclaimed, her blue eyes wide with excitement. "You were completely wrong about Bruce Patman. And I mean *completely*! Just ask these guys," she added, gesturing to her squadmates. "We just bumped into him in the hallway, and you should've *seen* the way he looked at me." She hugged herself, sighing. "It's obvious, Jessica—the guy's completely flipped over me! He and Regina Morrow are history."

Jessica looked skeptically at her friend. Though she usually defended Amy—especially to her twin sister Elizabeth—she had to admit that lately the girl had been getting worse. Amy really *did* seem boy-crazy these days. Ever since she'd gotten it into her head that Bruce Patman was in love with her, she'd been more and more difficult to deal with.

"It's true, Jessica," Maria Santelli agreed. The pert brunette opened her locker and took her cheerleading skirt out of her knapsack as she talked. "Believe me, I couldn't have imagined it either. I thought Bruce was as devoted to Regina as a guy could possibly be. But he really was fawning all over Amy. He seems hopelessly in love."

Jessica looked thoughtful as she turned from the mirror. Maria wasn't exactly given to overstatement in matters like this. Was it possible Amy wasn't just imagining the whole thing? Jessica narrowed her eyes at the blonde, trying to imagine what Bruce Patman might see in her. But then, she reminded herself, who could possibly tell what Bruce Patman saw in *anyone*? The only son of one of the richest families in the valley, Bruce had earned himself a reputation as the most arrogant boy around—until he fell in love with Regina Morrow, that is. If he was starting to get interested in Amy, he must be reverting to his old self.

Amy was certainly pretty. Tall and slender, with

soft blond hair cascading down to her shoulders, she had the willowy good looks of a cover girl. Lately Jessica had noticed that Amy seemed especially self-absorbed. All she seemed to talk about was the latest diet she'd discovered or special tricks to bring out the highlights in her hair. And since she and Bruce had been assigned to work together on a special project in their health class, her main interest in life—other than herself—was Bruce Patman.

Jessica could hardly believe how much she had heard from Amy about Bruce Patman over the past few days. In part she was getting sick of the subject. But her natural curiosity made her want to pump Amy for more information. Her friends Lila Fowler and Cara Walker would want to hear all about this, and Jessica hated to stop good gossip at its source.

"OK, OK," she said, relenting. "Tell me all about it."

"You know how it is," Amy said airily, grabbing a brush out of Maria's hand and setting to work on her hair. "You start working with someone—especially on an *intense* project like ours—and one thing kind of leads to another." She leaned forward, peering admiringly at herself in the mirror. "Naturally, Bruce is *very* attracted to me. I mean at first I could see how hard he was trying to restrain himself, but it was just too much—for both of us." She sighed. "I really admire Bruce for wanting to let Regina down easily. After all, you know how fragile she is—how temperamental. If he told her how he felt about me right away, who knows what she'd do?"

Jessica's eyes widened. "You really think things have gone so far that Bruce is going to dump Regina for you?"

Amy pouted. "Jessica, please," she objected. "You make it sound so heartless." She tossed her hair back and reached for a blue ribbon. "It's obvious that their relationship is over, that's all. Bruce has pretty much said so himself." She lowered her lashes, a scheming expression on her pretty face. "I don't want to push him or anything," she added. "After all, they've been together for a long time. But I do think it's inevitable that they're going to split up." She smiled knowingly. "And I intend to be right there for Bruce when they do!"

Jessica frowned. She was surprised that things had progressed so far between Bruce and Amy. Not that she'd ever had that much faith in Bruce as a person—in fact, there had been no love lost between Jessica and Bruce for quite some time now. But Regina really seemed to have changed Bruce. It was hard not to love Regina—everyone did. And though Jessica didn't see Regina as the "fragile" type—the way Amy had just described her—it was certainly true that Regina had been through quite a bit.

Regina Morrow was one of the most strikingly beautiful girls at school. Everything about her made her stand out—her raven black hair, her enormous blue eyes, her ivory complexion. But Regina's beauty wasn't the thing people remembered most about her.

She was sweet, soft-spoken, and somewhat shy—although once you got to know her, she had a delightfully warm sense of humor.

Elizabeth often remarked to Jessica that Regina's shyness might well be traced to the handicap she had overcome during the past year. Born with a severe hearing loss, Regina had attended special schools before entering Sweet Valley High in the middle of the junior year, and then had to work hard to be accepted. Treatments in Switzerland had given her almost normal hearing, but she still seemed to have a different quality—something that set her apart and made her unusual.

No one could believe it when Bruce and Regina fell in love. At first it seemed uncharacteristic for Bruce to fall for someone—especially someone as gentle and genuine as Regina. But their relationship was far from trouble-free. No sooner had they fallen in love than Regina was offered the opportunity to go to Switzerland and receive new treatments. Only after wrenching conflict did she decide to leave Bruce to undergo the procedures. Everyone assumed they would break up, but in fact they'd managed to survive the difficulties posed by a long-distance relationship. Jessica had assumed, as had all her classmates, that things were still going strong between them.

Until Amy Sutton had entered the picture.

But Jessica wasn't one to judge when it came to love. Her motto had always been, "Make sure you get what you want." She knew her twin would see it differently, but Jessica loved nothing better than a scandal. Her eyes sparkled now as she looked Amy up and down.

"You know," she said mischieviously, "things had been getting a little dull around here." She giggled. "I mean, people having to resort to using personal ads and everything." Jessica was referring to the ads that had been run in *The Oracle*, the school newspaper, which had generated a great deal of excitement and confusion over the past few weeks. "It sounds like you and Bruce are going to do your best to create some action!"

Amy gave her a smug little smile. "You're absolutely right," she said coolly. "I couldn't have put it any better myself."

"I don't get it," Elizabeth Wakefield said sharply, frowning at her twin as she rinsed some lettuce in the sink. The twins were in the Wakefields' Spanish-style kitchen, and Jessica was filling her sister in on the goings-on between Bruce and Amy while Elizabeth prepared a salad for dinner.

"I told you," Jessica said patiently, reaching over to snatch a piece of avocado. "Didn't you just hear what I said?"

"I did, but I can't believe Bruce would . . ." Elizabeth's voice trailed off as she stared at her twin. "I can't believe Amy Sutton," she added with irritation. "It sounds to me like she's completely out of line. She's wrong to be trying to worm her way into Bruce's affection, and she's certainly wrong to be telling all you guys about it!" She shook the lettuce dry, still frowning. "What if Regina hears about it from someone before Bruce talks to her? That is," she added, "if Amy's right and there really *is* something going on. It wouldn't surprise me if she's just made the whole thing up."

Jessica looked at Elizabeth with an expression halfway between frustration and concern. It was always this way when she tried to explain something perfectly simple to her sister. Elizabeth just couldn't seem to grasp the essentials. But that was because Elizabeth had such a fierce sense of right and wrong. Jessica took another piece of avocado, thinking how ironic it was that she and Elizabeth should look exactly alike. They were worlds apart when it came to their personalities!

Elizabeth was the older of the two by four minutes, and sometimes it seemed to Jessica that she took her role as "older" sister way too seriously. Not that Elizabeth meant to reprimand Jessica as much as she seemed to, but the truth was that Elizabeth was the more serious twin. She actually enjoyed things like homework and working long hours at *The Oracle*. She was incredibly loyal, and the things that mattered most to her—like her boyfriend, Jeffrey French, her best friend, Enid Rollins, her commitment to writing and schoolwork—absorbed her entirely. Jessica, however, was as changeable as the Pacific Ocean, full of energy and high spirits—and as inclined to get into trouble as her sister was inclined to stay out of it.

Nevertheless, the two looked like exact duplicates. With their five-foot-six-inch, model-slender figures and sun-streaked hair, they seemed to embody Southern California beauty. Every detail about them was identical, from the dimple each showed when she smiled to the gold lavaliere necklaces they wore—presents from their parents on their sixteenth birthday.

But right now Elizabeth's expression was considerably darker than her twin's. She liked and respected Regina Morrow quite a bit, and the thought of Amy Sutton trying to break up her relationship with Bruce really aggravated her.

The funny thing was that Amy had originally been Elizabeth's friend, not Jessica's. In sixth grade Elizabeth and Amy had been almost inseparable. When Amy's mother was offered a job as a broadcaster in Connecticut, the Suttons moved away, and eventually their friendship lapsed. Elizabeth had been delirious with joy when she learned that the Suttons were returning to Sweet Valley this year.

It had been quite a shock to see Amy again—the new Amy. The quiet tomboy was gone, and in her place Elizabeth found a spoiled, self-obsessed, boy-crazy girl who was manipulative rather than caring. Jessica—who had been less than thrilled at the prospect of Amy's return—was the one who ended up enjoying her company. In fact, Jessica had found her transformation a pleasant surprise. But then Jessica *liked* hours and hours of talk about hairstyles, fashion, and boys. Especially boys. And Elizabeth just didn't.

"I don't think it's necessarily such a bad thing," Jessica defended Amy, reaching for another piece of avocado.

Elizabeth slapped her hand lightly. "Save some of that for dinner, OK?" She scrutinized her twin with a searching look in her blue-green eyes. "Don't you care about Regina's feelings? I can't believe Bruce—even the old Bruce—would even consider giving up someone wonderful like Regina for Amy." She grimaced.

Jessica sighed. "Liz, I still can't see why you're so hard on Amy. Anyway, I don't think it's healthy for couples to stay together so long." She gave Elizabeth a meaningful stare. "I mean, what's the point of being young if you can't have lots of different experiences? Bruce and Regina have been together *forever*—even longer than you and Jeffrey."

"I'll try to ignore that," Elizabeth said lightly, taking ingredients for salad dressing out of the refrigerator. "I know how big you are on serious relationships, but even you have to admit that Regina's done Bruce a lot of good. If he *really* likes Amy . . ." She shuddered.

"Amy says it's because they've been thrown together so much on this health class project. They're supposed to be doing an oral report on drugs in Sweet Valley, and Amy says they're finding out all kinds of stuff. She says it's just *natural* that she and Bruce would end up feeling really strongly about each other."

Elizabeth groaned. "That makes absolutely no sense," she objected. "All I can say is that Bruce would be out of his mind to lose a great thing like his relationship with Regina." From her expression it was clear the discussion was over, as far as she was concerned. "Let's just hope he realizes that—and that Amy's just full of hot air. It sure wouldn't be the first time."

Jessica didn't answer. She was thinking that for such a smart girl, her twin could be pretty off-base at times like this.

She knew Amy Sutton well enough to know that when Amy wanted something, she got it. And clearly what Amy wanted right now was for Bruce Patman to tell Regina it was over between them forever.

Two

Amy Sutton was having the time of her life. It was a beautiful sunny afternoon, and she and Bruce were sitting together on the patio overlooking the Patmans' sprawling green estate, notes for their report spread out before them. But Amy was too intent on Bruce to be worried about their work. "I love this place," she gushed, putting her hand closer to his on the table. "Bruce, it's so much fun working together on this project." She looked meaningfully into his eyes. "Do you think it was fate that Mr. Jaworski assigned us to work together?"

Bruce laughed. "I don't think so. I think it may have been the seating chart that did it. It looks like Jaworski just went right down the rows when he assigned people to their partners."

Amy pouted. "I think it was fate," she murmured, inching her fingers closer to his.

Bruce reddened slightly, clearing his throat. "So . . . uh, do you think we're really going to be able to learn much about the drug situation in Sweet Valley from interviewing this cousin of yours?"

"Of course," Amy purred, her fingers almost touching his. "Mimi knows lots of people who know all about drugs. She'll be able to give us all the inside information we need." She lowered her voice, trying to make it sound husky. "I'm sure our report will be the best in the class."

Bruce looked down at her hand, obviously confused. "And you're sure the only time we can talk to her is tomorrow night?"

Amy nodded, trying to look very serious. Actually it had taken some effort to convince her cousin to meet with them on a Friday evening, but it seemed to Amy that she had to step up her efforts to win Bruce away from Regina. Getting him to work with her on a Friday night seemed a step in the right direction. It had worked the week before. Amy had insisted they work together, and Regina had been left at home . . . alone. There was a big Forties dance at school, and Amy heard from Lila Fowler that every one had commented on the fact that Bruce and Regina hadn't appeared together. The way Amy saw it, it wouldn't take much more time before she had Bruce doing what she wanted. She knew how much he liked her, and she had been thinking for weeks now about nothing else but how to get him to admit his feelings.

"You know, Bruce," she said meaningfully, shifting on her chair so that her knee bumped his under the table. "I had this amazing dream last night." She fixed her eyes intently on his. "I dreamed that you and I were out in the middle of nowhere together—just the two of us—and we were talking about our report, and all of a sudden . . ." She blushed, trying her hardest to look embarrassed. That summer spent studying acting back East was sure paying off now, she thought gratefully. Bruce looked positively mesmerized. "Oh, never mind," she said, pretending to be annoyed with herself. "Why am I bugging you with dumb personal stuff like my *dreams* when we have all this work to do?"

"No, go on," Bruce pleaded, fascinated. "What happened in the dream?"

Amy stared at his lips. "It's kind of embarrassing," she whispered, so caught up in her act that she almost forgot she was making the whole thing up as she went along.

Bruce cleared his throat, entranced. "Tell me," he begged. "I promise I won't hold it against you. It's only a dream, right?"

"Yeah," Amy said huskily, her knee against his again, "but remember what we learned in our psychology unit—don't some people think dreams represent wishes or something?"

Bruce stared at her. "Tell me what you dreamed," he repeated.

Amy took a deep breath. She had him exactly where she wanted him now, she thought triumphantly. "Well," she said softly, leaning closer to him, "we were, you know, in the middle of nowhere. And all of a sudden . . ." She gazed meaningfully up into his eyes. "All of a sudden you were kissing me." She blushed, dropping her eyes demurely. "See why I'm embarrassed?" she asked.

"Amy," Bruce said huskily, leaning forward and covering her hand with his. In the old days Bruce Patman would never have let an opportunity like this pass him by, and it was clear he was fighting now with his conscience.

Amy fixed her eyes quizzically on Bruce's. His lips were just inches from hers. If he just turned his head the slightest little bit . . .

"What if I told you that I really *do* want you to kiss me?" she whispered, still staring at him.

Bruce groaned. "Lord, Amy, you're completely irresistible," he muttered. Then he was bending forward, brushing her lips quickly with his. Amy slid her hand up behind his neck and pulled him closer as he started to straighten up again.

"A *real* kiss," she pouted. "Like this."

From the minute his lips touched hers, Amy knew she'd won the battle—*and* the war. There was no way Bruce was going to stay with Regina now. Not when he knew what it was like to be with someone who really wanted him the way she did!

"Amy," Bruce repeated, pulling back and staring at her with the old Bruce Patman "all I care about is what I want" look in his eyes. "I can't believe the way you kiss," he said, shaking his head and pulling her closer to him. "Who taught you how to kiss that way?"

Amy didn't answer immediately. She knew that what she said and did right then was incredibly important, and she wanted to make sure she didn't make a mistake. "We shouldn't see each other again," she whispered at last, avoiding his gaze. "I'm really sorry, Bruce. I had no business telling you about that dream. If Regina knew . . ."

Bruce frowned. "What do you mean, not see each other again? Are you kidding? Amy, I'm crazy about you!"

Amy paused, fiddling with the edge of her notebook. "But what about Regina?" she asked coyly. "I don't want to get between you two, Bruce. I couldn't stand that. Unless . . ." She let her voice trail off, still avoiding his eyes.

"Unless what?" Bruce prompted her.

"Unless you feel that things are almost over between you two," Amy said. "That would be different. Then I wouldn't feel so guilty about . . . you know, the way I feel about you."

Bruce tapped his fingers on the table. "I don't know how I feel," he said, frowning. "Until a couple of weeks ago I thought everything with Regina was perfect. But the more time I spend with you . . . the more time I spend thinking about you . . ." He gave her a cocky smile. "I'd kind of forgotten how much fun it is to spread the wealth—to share the old Bruce magic with more than one girl."

Amy let her fingers brush his again. "I'm putting you in a bad spot," she said, her voice filled with self-

15

reproach. "I'm forcing you to change your feelings toward Regina. And that's the last thing I want." She got to her feet, trying hard to look purposeful.

"Amy, don't leave!" Bruce moaned, grabbing her hand and staring at her with a pleading look on his handsome face. "I don't know what to do, but I'll figure something out. I'm sure I can convince Regina to let me do what I want. Anyway, I just know I've got to keep seeing you—that's all there is to it."

Amy sank back down in the chair, a triumphant little smile on her face as she pretended to study her notebook. She deserved an Academy Award for that performance, she thought with satisfaction.

And as for Regina Morrow, the girl had better get ready to face some bad news. Amy had Bruce where she wanted him, and she wasn't about to let him out of her clutches!

The next day, Friday, Amy could barely wait to meet Jessica at lunchtime and share her triumph with her best friend. "It was incredible," she declared, taking a miniscule spoonful of yogurt. "You should've seen the stars in Bruce's eyes when he kissed me!"

"So you really think he's going to break up with Regina?" Jessica asked.

"Of course they will," Amy scoffed, her blue eyes darkening. "And Bruce had better tell her soon," she added. "I don't mind being 'the other woman' for a little while, but it'll get boring soon. I want the whole world to know Bruce and I are in love. And I want

16

him to take me to the country club and buy me lots of expensive presents and stuff. How can he do that if he's still going out with Regina?"

"You've got a point." Jessica giggled. "Hey," she added, suddenly looking worried. "Liz and I were going to invite some people over tomorrow for a cookout. If we invite you *and* Regina, what's Bruce going to do?"

Amy shrugged. "It'll be fun to watch and see," she said, a manipulative smile on her face. "Actually, I think it'll do Bruce a lot of good to see us together. Don't you think I'm lots prettier than Regina is?" She watched Jessica anxiously for her reaction.

Jessica stared across the cafeteria at the table where Regina was sitting. "I don't know, Amy," she said honestly. "Regina's awfully pretty." Her eyes narrowed. "Hey, what's she doing eating lunch with Justin Belson? I didn't know they were friends."

Amy turned around and followed her gaze. "Who cares who Regina eats with—as long as it isn't Bruce?" she said airily. "I think you're wrong, Jess. That dress makes her hips look big. And she's way too pale. She looks like the sort of girl you'd want to bring home to meet your parents—not the sort of girl who can really make your pulse race."

Jessica groaned. "I think you've been watching too much TV. You're starting to sound like a perfume commercial." She was still eyeing Justin Belson with interest. "The last I heard, Justin was on academic probation," she remarked. "He isn't exactly Regina's type. He hangs out with Molly Hecht and Jan Brown and that whole crowd."

"Yeah, Molly Hecht is trouble," Amy agreed. "My cousin Mimi saw her at a party in L.A. last weekend that got busted by the police. Two of the college guys got arrested for having cocaine."

Jessica's eyes widened. "You think Molly and Justin are mixed up with drugs?" she demanded.

Amy shrugged. "I honestly don't know. And to tell you the truth, Jess, I just don't care." She leaned forward, her blue eyes shining. "All I care about is making sure that Bruce leaves your house tomorrow night with *me* and not with Regina! If you've got any ideas on how to make that happen, promise you'll let me know."

"I promise," Jessica murmured. But she was barely listening. She was watching Regina and Justin, who were apparently deep in conversation. What on earth could they have to talk to each other about? she wondered. It made her uneasy, though she couldn't exactly say why.

Jessica just hoped Regina knew that Justin and his crowd were bad news. And that she knew enough to stay far away from him.

Regina Morrow was confused. Everything seemed to have gone wrong that day. First of all, Bruce had cancelled their plans to go to the country club that night—saying he had to work with Amy on their project again. He *said* the only possible time he and Amy could talk to the people at the drug rehabilitation center downtown was at seven-thirty, and that they had agreed to meet Amy's cousin afterward to get some inside information on the drug situation at the college she went to. Regina believed him, but she couldn't help feeling disappointed. It was the second Friday night in a row in which their plans had been interrupted by Amy Sutton.

And then Bruce had stood her up for lunch! They were supposed to meet right here, at their usual table, but he just hadn't showed. At ten past twelve, Regina had gone through the line by herself and taken her tray back to the table. That was when Justin had come over. "Can I join you?" he asked, a shy smile on his face.

Regina had looked up in surprise. She didn't know Justin at all. A tall, slender boy with auburn hair and chiseled, attractive features, he seemed to spend most of his time alone—or with a crowd she barely knew. "Sure," she said after a slight hesitation. Why not? Bruce clearly wasn't going to meet her, and she hated to eat alone.

"I've seen you eat here every day, and I've always wanted to say hello," Justin told her. He had a nice voice—very low and soft. "But you're always with that guy Bruce. Is he your boyfriend?"

Regina nodded. "Are you a junior? I don't think we've ever met before, have we? I'm Regina Morrow."

"Justin Belson," he said, putting his hand out to shake. "Yeah, I'm a junior. But I should be a senior.

19

I took a year off when . . ." His voice trailed off. "I had some family problems so I took a little time off." He smiled at her, a crooked, disarming smile that made Regina feel a strange twinge of sympathy. "I've always known who you are, though. You're the one who had your picture on the cover of *Ingenue* magazine." He grinned. "I've got three copies at home. I'm one of your biggest fans."

Regina blushed. "That was a total fluke," she assured him. "I was just downtown one day and the man who runs Townsend Modeling Agency saw me and thought I looked right for this contest they were having. You know—sort of fresh and girlish." She smiled. "Not sophisticated and glamorous, like their models usually are."

"You do look fresh," Justin said seriously, his brown eyes intent. "You look . . ." He paused, searching for the right word. "Good," he finished, slightly helpless.

Regina laughed. "I guess I am good—if you mean studious, well-behaved, all that sort of stuff." She eyed him curiously. "Aren't you?"

"Me? Good?" Justin looked at her, his thin shoulders slightly hunched. Regina thought he was very handsome, in a way that she found puzzling—and slightly disturbing. "Not really," he said at last. "Hey, listen. I've got tickets to a basketball game in L.A. tonight. You interested?"

Regina stared at him. Was he asking her out?

"Uh . . . I'm sorry, but I don't think Bruce would really like it. I mean—"

"I understand," Justin said quickly. "I didn't mean to embarrass you," he added, seeing her blush. "I just really hoped we could get to know each other better. But maybe tonight isn't the right time. Can we have lunch again one day next week?"

"Sure," Regina said. She didn't see what harm it could do. Justin seemed really nice, and she thought it would be fun to get to know him.

In fact, a tiny nagging voice inside her was asking why she'd turned him down for that evening. What else was she going to do—sit around and wait for Bruce and Amy to finish what they were doing?

But she checked the disloyal thought at once. Bruce couldn't help having to work on a Friday every once in a while. And she admired him for having chosen to do his report on something as important as drug abuse.

It was just that she couldn't help feeling uneasy about Amy Sutton.

Three

"I don't get it, Jess," Elizabeth said with a sigh. The girls were sitting out by the Wakefields' in-ground swimming pool, making a grocery list for their barbecue that evening. Jessica had just been telling her sister that she couldn't wait for the cookout. "There's bound to be lots of scandal," she said. "Especially since all three members of the Love Triangle are coming."

That was what Elizabeth couldn't understand— how her sister could actually relish the prospect of a romantic World War Three. "Explain to me why you're looking forward to it," she pleaded. "I just don't see what's going to be fun about watching Regina's heart break."

Jessica sighed patiently. "What fun would it be if nothing exciting happened? Face it, Liz. Happy couples are boring. Didn't some famous novel start off about that?"

"That was happy families, not happy couples," Eliz-

22

abeth corrected her. "And Tolstoy didn't say they were boring—just that they were *alike*."

Jessica yawned. "Well, happy couples are *boring*. Bruce has gotten really dull since he met Regina. Granted he was a pain before, but lately all he does is follow her around like a little puppy. I think his interest in Amy is a healthy sign."

"Oh, you do," Elizabeth retorted. "That's just great, Jess. And I suppose you think it's 'healthy' that poor Regina Morrow hasn't got the faintest idea that Bruce has been two-timing her behind her back? And that she's going to show up tonight at *our* party and have to watch Amy fawning all over him?"

Jessica considered for a minute. "I don't think we should leave out the potato chips and dip," she said finally, clearly avoiding her sister's penetrating gaze. "And I think we need hot dogs *and* hamburgers. You don't want to starve our guests, do you?"

Elizabeth shook her head. "OK, let's drop it," she said, frowning. She could tell she wasn't going to get Jessica to talk seriously about Regina and Bruce—at least not as long as the conversation stayed vague. "I wonder if I should talk to Regina," she mused, watching her twin out of the corner of her eye for a reaction.

"What do you mean, 'talk to Regina'?" Jessica demanded, looking a little worried.

"Well, I just don't think it's fair that she's the only one who's totally in the dark about Bruce and Amy. You said Lila knew about it, right?"

"Yes," Jessica admitted grudgingly. "So?"

"And the other cheerleaders know, right?"

Jessica shrugged. "I guess so. What's the big deal? Regina will find out sooner or later. From the way Amy was making it sound yesterday at lunch, Bruce has practically sworn he's going to break up with her—the first chance he gets. At least that's what Amy seems to think."

"Well, I don't think it's fair. I think I should warn Regina before she comes over tonight. After all, she considers me one of her best friends. Isn't it my obligation to tell her what a rat Bruce is being?"

Jessica's aquamarine eyes flew wide open. "Are you insane?" she squealed. "If you tell Regina, she'll go right to Bruce. And *he'll* go right to Amy. And guess who Amy will go right to?"

Elizabeth looked at her calmly. "I take it Amy doesn't know you've told me," she said dryly.

Jessica bit her lip. "She doesn't," she admitted. "And, Liz, you can't tell Regina—you just can't! Amy would murder me. She doesn't want to pressure Bruce. If you say something to Regina, it'll be obvious how you found out. Promise you won't say a word."

Elizabeth studied the grocery list with thoughtful eyes. "I can't promise that," she said gravely. "Not when I don't know yet what's right." She relented when she saw how miserable her twin looked. "But I'll certainly consider your point of view," she teased her.

Jessica didn't smile. In fact she was positively glowering by the time they had completed the shopping list. That was all she needed—for Elizabeth to decide to get all high and mighty and blab the whole story to Regina before the barbecue.

Amy would kill her—absolutely *kill* her. If there was one thing Jessica was familiar with, it was Amy Sutton's wrath. If it was at all possible, she wanted to keep her sister from saying a single word to Regina.

"What would you do if you were in my situation?" Elizabeth asked Jeffrey French. It was late Saturday afternoon, and she and Jeffrey were on the beach, soaking up the last strong rays and watching the surfers.

Jeffrey frowned, his green eyes serious. Elizabeth loved the way he looked when he was concentrating hard—as he was just then. His forehead wrinkled up a little bit, and he seemed even cuter than usual. But then, Jeffrey always looked cute to her, with his blond hair and lively green eyes. Elizabeth loved being with him. He was serious and dependable, but at the same time he was lots of fun—so things never got boring with him, despite what Jessica had said about happy couples.

"I'm not sure what I'd do," Jeffrey said thoughtfully. "I can see both sides of the argument. On the one hand I can see why you feel as if you owe it to Regina to tell her what's going on. It does seem pretty rotten that so many people know about it when Regina hasn't got a clue. Especially since it looks as if things are going to come to a head tonight, one way or another.

If Regina comes with absolutely no warning . . . it could be terrible. Think how humiliated she'll feel!"

"I know. That's exactly what's worrying me," Elizabeth agreed. "And if she finds out that I knew beforehand, won't she feel like I've betrayed her by keeping quiet?"

Jeffrey thought it over for a minute. "On the other hand—and I hate to say this, Liz, but I think it's true—there's a real risk involved in saying something. First of all, it's possible the whole thing could blow over. More than possible, if you ask me. Amy's probably exaggerating, and who knows whether or not Bruce really plans to break up with Regina? So if you tell her, you might actually be responsible for a huge confrontation. And you wouldn't want that. Also, Regina might be furious with you for being the bearer of bad news."

"You're right." Elizabeth sighed uneasily. "I'm afraid it looks bad whatever I do." She looked long and hard at Jeffrey. "Suppose it were you," she said thoughtfully. "I mean suppose—just for the sake of it—that *you* started feeling something for someone else. I wonder if I'd want someone else to tell me about it."

Jeffrey looked horror-stricken. "Liz, I would *never* do that to you," he exclaimed, pulling her close to him. "I don't even like talking about it," he added, his voice muffled against her hair.

Elizabeth sighed. "I know," she said huskily. "Me neither. The truth is, though, that I think I'd rather wait and hear it from you. I wouldn't want someone like Enid to break it to me."

Jeffrey stared out at the ocean. "I think you should wait and see what happens," he said finally. "It really is between Bruce and Regina. Hard as it is to keep quiet, I think we ought to mind our own business."

Elizabeth nodded. It seemed that saying something to Regina would be unfair. She just hoped Jeffrey was right about Amy's having exaggerated the extent of her involvement with Bruce. Maybe there was still a chance it would all blow over and everything would be OK.

"Regina—telephone!" Nicholas called from his bedroom.

Regina put down her hairbrush and frowned at her reflection. "I've got it!" she called back. She waited to hear her brother hang up, but for some reason he didn't.

"Regina? It's Justin Belson. I was wondering if you felt like going to see a movie or something tonight."

Regina raised her eyebrows, surprised. Just then she heard the click as her brother hung up the receiver. "I . . . uh, I'm really sorry, Justin. But I've got plans," she said rapidly. "Bruce and I are going over to a friend's house for a barbecue."

Justin paused. "That sounds fun," he said. Was it her imagination or did his voice sound slightly wistful? "What about tomorrow—are you doing anything tomorrow?" he asked.

Regina twisted the telephone cord between her fingers. Somehow she felt it wasn't right to make plans with Justin. Not that Bruce was the jealous type—because he wasn't. They trusted each other. But she got the impression that Justin liked her, and she thought it would be wrong to encourage him. "I'm sorry, Justin," she said politely, "but I have an awful lot of homework. Maybe we can have lunch together next week like you suggested in the cafeteria yesterday."

"OK," Justin said. "Well, have fun tonight."

"Thanks," Regina said. She was going to add something, but before she got the chance, he'd hung up.

The next minute Nicholas knocked on her door, poking his head in with an inquisitive look on his face. "Was that really Justin Belson?" he demanded.

Regina remembered then that Nicholas had taken longer than usual to hang up his extension. "Yes," she said, slightly annoyed. She adored her older brother, but sometimes Nicholas could be overprotective. His handsome face was set in a frown just then, and she sensed an interrogation coming.

"Since when are you friends with Justin?" Nicholas continued, crossing his arms over his chest and scowling at her with a big-brother-knows-best look on his face. "My friend Sam Watson went out with a girl once who was friends with him. He doesn't seem like someone you'd want to be close to."

"We're not really friends," Regina said slowly. She didn't like her brother's tone, and she began to change her mind as she spoke. "I just met him this week," she added defensively. "He's a perfectly nice guy, Nicholas. You don't need to give me that look—I'm old enough to take care of myself."

"Well, according to Sam, Justin Belson is bad news," Nicholas declared. "In fact, his name just came up this morning because Sam was telling me about the new probation rules the school administration came up with. You know Justin's on academic probation for cutting class so many times, don't you? And what about that group he hangs out with? That girl Molly Hecht always seems to be in some kind of scrape. Some of those kids—like Jan Brown—are into drugs in a big way. Do yourself a favor and just drop this Belson character right now."

Regina's eyes flashed. "Incidentally," she snapped, "since when do you listen in on my phone calls?"

Nicholas glared. "I wasn't listening in. I just happen to care about what happens to you, that's all. And I know for a fact that this guy is trouble. I don't want you hanging around with him."

Regina heard her mother's footsteps on the stairs, and her jaw began to tremble. She didn't want her mother to hear their argument. "Let's just drop it," she muttered. But it was too late.

"What's going on?" Mrs. Morrow asked as she came up from the landing. She looked from Nicholas to Regina with surprise, her pretty face concerned. At thirty-eight Skye Morrow was as beautiful as she had been the day she shot her last assignment as a top-fashion model in New York. But her expression was troubled as she looked from her son to her daughter. She wasn't used to hearing her children argue.

"Nothing," Regina said quickly.

But Nicholas wasn't going to let her off the hook. "I was just explaining to Regina that this guy Justin Belson is bad news. I don't want to see her get mixed up with a bad crowd."

"Who's Justin Belson? And why would you want to get involved with a bad crowd, honey? I thought you were so busy lately with Bruce and your other friends."

"I'm not involved with a bad crowd, Mom," Regina said patiently, giving her brother a murderous look. "Nicholas is just making a mountain out of a molehill. This guy just called to say hello, that's all. And he's nice—there's nothing wrong with him!"

"If your brother thinks he's wrong for you, darling, I'm sure there's no point encouraging him," Mrs. Morrow said evenly, patting Regina on the shoulder as if the matter were settled once and for all. Regina could feel herself getting angry, but she couldn't see the point of making a scene. After all, Nicholas *was* trying to protect her, and it wasn't as if she were all that eager to get to know Justin anyway.

Besides, it was getting late, and she had to get ready to go to the Wakefields' barbecue. She felt like she'd barely seen or spoken to Bruce in days. In fact, she hadn't even gotten a chance to find out where he'd been at lunchtime the day before when this whole thing with Justin had gotten started.

Clearly this wasn't the time to argue with Nicholas and her mother about Justin Belson. They all had more important things to think about. And the thing Regina was thinking about was Bruce.

Why hadn't he called to tell her what time he was picking her up? He hadn't been calling just to talk anymore either.

Suddenly Regina was worried about Bruce. Really worried. She couldn't wait to see him to find out that everything was still all right.

Four

"Look," Regina said, staring hard at Bruce, "I don't mean to sound like a nagging housewife or something. I just feel really confused. It isn't like you to forget about a lunch date—and it isn't like you not to call either."

Regina and Bruce were sitting together in his black Porsche in front of the Wakefields' house, getting ready to go join the rest of the group in the backyard. It was late afternoon and still warm, but Regina felt shivery—as if something bad were about to happen. Bruce just wasn't acting at all like himself. He looked great in a white polo shirt and chinos, but he seemed to be avoiding her gaze. She couldn't understand why he was being so uncommunicative.

"I'm sorry about lunch. But I told you—Amy and I had to run to the public library downtown to do some quick fact-checking." Bruce ran a hand through his hair, frowning. "This stuff is amazing, Regina. You wouldn't believe some of the information Amy's found out about the availability of speed and cocaine—even in middle schools around here! It's incredible. Her cousin Mimi says that—"

"Look," Regina said, cutting him off, "I may be making too much out of nothing, but you two seem to be spending an awful lot of time together lately. In fact—"

"We should go in, Regina," Bruce interrupted. "We don't want to be rude to the Wakefields."

Regina bit her lip, her face unhappy. Bruce got out of the car, slamming his door shut, and she had no choice but to follow him. The prospect of making small talk with her friends suddenly seemed unappealing. Regina wished she and Bruce could just sit down together and talk—really talk. She felt apprehensive and unhappy, though she couldn't exactly say why.

But this was hardly the time or place for a confrontation. Jessica was hurrying toward them with a welcoming smile as they walked around to the back of the house, where the cookout was taking place.

"Bruce! Regina! We were just talking about you two," Jessica declared. "We were trying to decide who's best at grilling hamburgers, and Roger started telling everyone that his cousin is the California state champion when it comes to barbecuing."

Roger Patman was Bruce's first cousin. He and his girlfriend, Olivia Davidson, were among the guests at the Wakefields' that afternoon. From the grateful expression on Bruce's face when Jessica teased him about his cooking skills, she guessed he wouldn't mind the chance to get away from Regina just then.

"I'd be glad to help," he said cheerfully. "Regina, would you mind? Though I'm much better at grilling steaks," he added, with a characteristic "money is no object" grin.

Jessica rolled her eyes. "I'm sure you are," she said, watching him lope off toward the crowd in the backyard. She turned to Regina with an inquisitive look in her eyes. "How are you, Regina? I haven't seen you around much lately."

Regina followed Bruce with her gaze, a shadow crossing her pretty face. "I'm fine," she said briefly. "Is there anything *I* can do to help?"

"Just come with me," Jessica instructed, leading Regina toward the patio, where a dozen or so girls were sipping cool drinks and talking animatedly. The boys were playing Frisbee on the lawn—all but Bruce, who was studying the charcoals with a scowl on his face.

Winston Egbert, whose silly pranks had won him the reputation of being the clown of the junior class, wanted the Frisbee game to get more competitive. "Frisbee baseball!" he hollered to Ken Matthews. "Ken, you play first. I'll pitch."

Jeffrey gave Elizabeth a quick kiss as he sprinted over to take up a position at what had just been declared third base. Elizabeth and Jessica exchanged grins. The barbecue was getting off to a perfect start.

It was a beautiful afternoon. The sunlight had turned golden, but it was still warm, and the smell of smoking coals permeated the air, making everyone's appetite quicken.

Regina sat down at the patio table, looking around shyly at the others. It was funny how often she still felt uncomfortable at situations like this, where everyone else was so natural—so clearly having fun. This may have been partly due to years and years at "special" schools before she attended Sweet Valley. She still felt like an outsider at times, as if she were still deaf, still reacting to life differently from the others. Moreover, she had always been a little shy. And she hadn't spent all that much time with her class—she'd entered Sweet Valley High after school had already started, and between that and her months in Switzerland, she really felt out of synch.

Not that the group here wasn't friendly. Regina looked around the table with a shy smile. Olivia Davidson was really nice—a shy, slightly "artsy" girl who dated Bruce's cousin Roger. She liked Olivia. Next to Olivia was Caroline Pearce, a pixyish redhead with an animated, welcoming personality. She was sweet—and lots of fun. Cara Walker, one of Jessica's best friends, was next in the circle. Cara was a lovely, good-natured girl who had mellowed considerably since she fell in love with Steven Wakefield, the twins' older brother. Lila Fowler was on Cara's right. There was no love lost between Lila and Regina, true enough—Lila was incredibly jealous of Regina, and seemed to take every opportunity to compete. But even Lila seemed in a relaxed, friendly mood tonight.

She knew the other girls at the table less well—with the exception of Enid Rollins, Elizabeth's best friend—a smart, down-to-earth girl whom Regina liked. Regina knew Maria Santelli, Winston's girlfriend, only from having been introduced once or twice. In fact, Maria seemed to be staring at her curiously—or was it her imagination? Regina blushed and looked away.

"Hey, guys!" a familiar voice called. Everyone looked up. It was Amy Sutton, hurrying across the lawn, looking like a model in a fashion layout in a white sundress and cotton espadrilles. Regina felt her pulse quicken. She didn't know Amy had been invited. It made sense, of course. Amy was a good friend of Jessica's. There was no reason to feel strange about it, she chided herself. It wasn't as if—

But her thoughts were interrupted as she and the others watched Amy turn to look at Bruce, who was standing, absolutely frozen, by the barbecue, now that the Frisbee game was over. Their gazes locked and Amy smiled—a tiny, knowing smile that made Regina's stomach feel suddenly queasy. It lasted only an instant—Amy standing in a pool of late afternoon sunlight, eyes wide, staring at Bruce, and Bruce staring back at her. Then the connection was broken. Amy came over to join them all at the table, and Bruce, eyes downcast, fiddled with the grill. But Regina felt as though something devastating had happened.

Bruce and Amy, she thought miserably. That was what had been bothering her all day—all week, in fact. That explained the peculiar premonitions she'd been having. She was worried about Bruce and Amy.

"I'm starving," Amy announced to the tableful of girls, plopping down on a chair between Lila and Jessica. "I've been running around all day with my cousin Mimi, trying to get more information on this drug stuff." She wrinkled her nose, helping herself to a handful of potato chips. "I don't see how anyone can get involved in that junk."

Lila yawned. "I'd much rather talk about food than about your drug report. I'm really hungry," she said, stretching luxuriously. "What on earth is Bruce doing to those hamburgers?"

"I'll go help him," Amy said immediately, jumping to her feet and hurrying over to the barbecue. Lila raised her eyebrows and gave Cara and Jessica a meaningful look, and Maria Santelli coughed. Regina felt her face redden. Did everyone know something she didn't?

She tried to look as if nothing were wrong, but it was hard not to turn and watch Amy. OK, maybe volunteering to help barbecue wasn't such a big deal. But did she have to stand so close to Bruce? Did she have to keep putting her hand on his arm?

Regina felt close to tears, but she swore to herself that she wasn't going to show how uncomfortable and upset she was. Not in front of the others. Besides, she had never mistrusted Bruce in the past, and she wasn't going to now. Not until she'd gotten a chance to ask him exactly what was going on between Amy and him.

Elizabeth shook the match out over the candle she had just lit. The barbecue was a terrific success. Everyone had eaten till they were completely stuffed, and by now the mood of the party had mellowed as it got darker outside. Olivia was playing the guitar, and a small group had gathered around her, singing songs. Winston, Maria, Enid, and Ken were telling ghost stories out by the pool, and other groups of two or three people were scattered around the yard, talking in low voices or just lying back and looking up at the stars.

Elizabeth turned to Jeffrey. "Where's Bruce?" she asked anxiously. "Regina's sitting out by the pool all by herself."

"Uh-oh," Jeffrey said, turning to scan the yard. "Amy isn't here either," he murmured, putting his hand on Elizabeth's. "I hope they haven't disappeared somewhere together. That's all we need."

Elizabeth felt her face getting hot. "I'm ready to kill both of them," she said in a low, angry voice. "I don't see how they can possibly act the way they've been acting in front of Regina. I mean, it's obvious—at least as far as Amy's concerned—what's going on. She was following him around all evening, with that sick little 'I love you so much and I'm trying to hide it but I can't' look in her eyes."

Jeffrey sighed. "I'm just waiting for Regina to explode. She's obviously upset. And I'm sure it doesn't make it any easier feeling like all of us know what's going on."

Elizabeth grabbed Jeffrey's hand. "Look," she said. "Isn't that Bruce over there—behind the pine tree?"

Jeffrey squinted through the dusk at the huge tree in the distance. "Uh-oh," he said. "He isn't alone either. He and Amy couldn't resist each other even long enough for him to take Regina home."

Elizabeth jumped to her feet, her face burning. "I'm going to go distract Regina," she told Jeffrey. "Why don't you see if you can't separate them? Tell Bruce he can carry on with Amy someplace else—but not here. Not when Regina's right here."

A minute later she had crossed the lawn to the pool-side, where Regina was fidgeting nervously on a deck chair, looking around with a perplexed, unhappy expression on her face. "Have you seen Bruce?" she asked Elizabeth directly. "I'm not feeling all that well. I kind of want to go home and go to sleep."

"I haven't seen him," Elizabeth lied, feeling terrible as she looked down at her friend's miserable face. She wanted to tell Regina the truth. It didn't seem to matter anymore that Bruce hadn't told her, that it was over between Bruce and Regina. Elizabeth felt as if she owed it to her friend to tell her the truth. But she couldn't imagine saying anything right then and there. Not with everyone else around. "Come on," she said gently, putting her hand on Regina's shoulder. "I'll drive you home."

Regina got to her feet woodenly. "I should wait for

Bruce," she began. Just then her eyes widened as she stared across the lawn at the spot where Jeffrey was emerging from behind the pine tree in the back of the Wakefields' lot. Bruce and Amy were right behind him, looking sheepish.

Elizabeth followed Regina's gaze.

"You knew where he was all along," Regina said in a choked voice. "You all knew. Why didn't you tell me, Liz? I thought you were my friend."

Elizabeth gulped, not knowing what to say. It was impossible to keep lying, though. "I didn't think it was up to me," she murmured, putting her hand on Regina's arm. "Let me take you home," she begged. "I'm sorry I didn't say anything. I just wanted to keep you from getting hurt."

Regina's face was dead white. "Let go of me," she seethed, jerking back when she felt Elizabeth's touch. "I thought you were my friend," she repeated, her voice so cold and angry that she sounded like a stranger. "You all knew," she added furiously. "You knew, and you let me come here and make a fool of myself!"

Elizabeth's eyes filled with tears. "Regina, please let me try to explain," she began. But it was too late.

Regina stormed across the lawn, her dark hair flying. "Don't give me that look," she snapped at Bruce. "I want your car keys. I'm taking the Porsche, and I'm going to drive it to my house. Come pick it up whenever you want it—the keys will be in the mailbox." Her face was still ashen and she was trembling

Five

At first when Regina woke up on Sunday morning, she couldn't remember what had happened. Then all the miserable events of the night before came flooding back to her. Finding out about Amy and Bruce. Coming back to the house and calling Justin. She sighed, rolling over and pushing her face into her pillow. Usually Regina loved Sunday mornings. None of the Morrows got up until pretty late, and then the one rule was: no noise. Everyone just lazed around over breakfast with the newspaper and waited to see how the day would unfold.

Well, Regina knew this Sunday would be different. It would be her first Sunday without Bruce.

She realized now that what had happened last night had been a long time in coming. Couples didn't just break up with no warning. The truth was that Amy Sutton wasn't the real source of the problem. Of course, it was clear that Bruce had completely fallen

43

for her, but Regina had to admit she'd seen trouble coming for weeks.

Bruce had never had a long-term commitment before he'd met her. Quite the opposite, in fact. He'd always enjoyed the pursuit more than the capture, and dating one pretty, desirable girl after another had been part of the old Bruce Patman image—the image that compelled him to get license plates for his car that read: 1 BRUCE 1. Regina was something entirely new for him, and she suspected now that the novelty of their relationship had appealed to him a great deal. Being in love—when it was for the first time—was incredibly exciting, and Bruce had thrown himself into their relationship with terrific zeal. She knew that he'd really loved her too. He had been faithful to her the whole time she was in Switzerland, and had stood by her through some tough times—including the dreadful episode when she had been forced onto a plane at gunpoint and brought back to Sweet Valley to be held hostage in her parents' home.

But Regina also knew that their relationship had been punctuated with high drama. No sooner had they declared their love, than they were separated. The long-distance romance had been difficult, but since both of them had enough money for phone calls, they managed to stay in touch. And transatlantic romance was exciting. There had been plenty of intrigue to keep their relationship fresh. Then, when Regina came back, there was the excitement of her cure—she could hear Bruce's voice for the first time, and it almost seemed as if their relationship began afresh.

Only in the past few months had they had to adjust to the ordinary ups and downs of a normal romantic relationship. Regina had sensed there might be difficulties involved. Frankly, she thought Bruce was getting a little bored. He was less excited at the prospect of a quiet Friday evening alone with her than he might have been earlier on. Sometimes she caught him staring off into space with a restless expression on his face. She, in turn, had become more withdrawn, less able to express what was on her mind. As she felt him withdraw, she felt herself—despite her best intentions—becoming clingier and more demanding. Months ago she wouldn't have minded in the least if Bruce had spent a night out with his friends. But his behavior made her so insecure lately that she'd changed too—becoming much more dependent on him and much less fun.

As for Amy . . . well, Regina ached every time she thought of Bruce with her, but she could certainly see why Bruce was attracted to the girl. Amy was exactly like the girls he had dated before Regina—fluffy, silly, flirtatious—fun for a while, and impossible to take seriously.

Rationally it all made sense to Regina. But emotionally . . . well, she couldn't accept it. She felt devastated by Bruce's behavior, as if he'd betrayed her so fundamentally that she never wanted to face him again. Lying in bed and mulling through the events of the prior evening, she was doubly glad she had agreed to go out with Justin that night. She needed to take her mind off Bruce and Amy—and fast.

Regina had made a resolution the night before, after she and Justin had decided to meet some of his friends in town. She had resolved not to talk to Bruce when he called—which she knew he would. He would probably have dozens of excuses for his behavior the night before. Knowing Bruce's reputation, he might even want to keep stringing her along while he got to know Amy better. But Regina wasn't going to be part of Bruce's games. She'd never had her heart broken before, and she didn't exactly know the rules. But she knew she couldn't bear to talk to him. It would be hard enough having to face him in school, but she'd already decided that the one thing she could salvage was her pride. No one was going to know how much she was suffering. And Justin Belson would fit nicely into that scheme.

"How was the barbecue?" Mrs. Morrow asked when Regina wandered into the cozy breakfast room. Nicholas was deeply absorbed in the sports section and barely glanced up at her as she slid into a chair across from him.

"Fine," Regina said briefly, pouring herself a glass of milk. "Can I have the fashion section, please?"

"Bruce called while you were in the shower," her mother continued. "He said he wants to come by to get the car, and that he really wants to talk to you. He'll call back in a little while."

Regina raised one eyebrow and turned to the newspaper. She sensed her mother's curiosity was piqued, but she didn't want to encourage any questions.

Nicholas suddenly seemed to forget about the basketball scores he'd been studying. "I heard you two had sort of a misunderstanding," he said, reaching for a piece of toast.

Regina's eyes flashed. "How did you hear that? Doesn't anyone in this town have anything better to do than to talk about Bruce and me?"

"Hey," Nicholas said affably. "Calm down! I just happened to bump into Ken Matthews when I was out jogging this morning, that's all. And he said—"

Regina put her hands over her ears. "Stop," she said, her eyes glistening with tears.

Mrs. Morrow stared at her, concerned. "Honey, was this a serious argument? Bruce didn't sound as if anything were wrong on the phone."

"Well, something *is* wrong," Regina said, trying to seem very busy about buttering a piece of toast. "We broke up," she added noncommittally. "And I think it's high time too. We're too young to get so serious."

Nicholas, who had occasionally suggested pretty much the same thing to his younger sister, looked at her with consternation. "Are you sure? I thought you two were like Romeo and Juliet or something."

"Yeah, and look what happened to them," Regina snapped. She knew she was being touchy, but she wanted the discussion to end. It hurt too much to talk about it.

"What should I say if he calls back, honey?" her

47

mother demanded when Regina got up from the table.

"Tell him I'm not home," Regina suggested. All she had to do to stay angry was to conjure up the image of Bruce and Amy coming out from behind that pine tree together, hand in hand. "Or better yet, tell him I don't want to talk to him. Ever again!"

With that she spun on her heel and dashed out of the room. It was going to be a long time before she could tolerate hearing Bruce's name. Until then she was just going to have to do everything she could to keep herself busy so she wouldn't go crazy with grief.

And Justin Belson seemed to be the obvious answer.

"I've never been here before," Regina said, swallowing nervously. Kelly's was a notorious dive in Sweet Valley—a place where kids in trouble liked to go because it was rumored that the bar would serve anyone, even teenagers, as long as they could pay for their drinks. Regina knew her parents would die if they could see her now. For one thing, Justin wasn't exactly dressed the way most of the boys her age dressed. He was wearing a leather jacket, and even with his chiseled features, he looked slightly tough— a little older than guys she knew at school, and definitely more streetwise. Her own outfit—a pair of black jeans and a loose cotton sweater—looked schoolgirlish next to his. But Justin didn't seem to mind. He looked at her with a mixture of admiration and . . . well, something she couldn't quite put her finger on. Something like *awe*.

"You've never been to Kelly's?" Justin repeated incredulously. "You're kidding! Boy, you really *have* led a sheltered life."

Regina followed him into the dimly lit bar, blinking nervously as she looked around her. It looked pretty normal, actually. There was an old jukebox in the corner, and the guy behind the bar was polishing glasses, like bartenders always seemed to do in movies. One or two men were sitting at the bar, but otherwise the place was quiet. But then, it was a Sunday evening.

"Let me buy you a beer," Justin said, taking a seat in a booth and looking at her intently.

"Uh, no thanks. I'd like a Coke," Regina said uncomfortably as she sat opposite Justin.

Justin laughed, shrugged at the waiter, and leaned back in the booth. "Make that one Coke and one beer," he said. The waiter nodded, and Regina chewed on the corner of her lip. What if he got drunk? Should she ask to drive home? She felt her palms begin to sweat. Maybe she shouldn't have come. Her parents didn't even know where she was—she'd sneaked out, saying she was going over to Elizabeth's to study.

Justin seemed to sense she was nervous. "You're not used to places like this, are you?" he said. His voice sounded wistful. When Regina shook her head, he added, "Next time we'll go somewhere *you* choose. I just didn't think, that's all."

Regina relaxed slightly. He was *nice*. "Don't your parents mind about stuff like drinking?" she asked.

Justin stared at her. "My parents," he repeated bitterly. Regina guessed she had hit a nerve. "Look," Justin added, "I don't want to go on and on about my family. It's too depressing. But I guess I should tell you that my father's dead. He got killed two years ago—the year I took off school."

Regina stared. "Killed? You mean—"

"Murdered," Justin said, sighing heavily. "It's straight out of a B-grade cops-and-robbers film. Only it really happened. My dad owned a liquor store on Putnam Avenue, which isn't the greatest part of town. He'd done pretty well with it, though, and business was OK. Up until then I guess he and Mom and I were your basic old family. And then . . ." He spread his hands, a grimace on his handsome face. "Boom. The whole thing exploded in our faces."

"What happened?" Regina demanded, her eyes big.

"Dad got mugged by two stupid kids trying to rip him off for drug money. They weren't even as old as we are now," he added, looking away from her. The waiter brought their drinks, and Justin was quiet for a minute, pushing the beer glass back and forth on the table. "Anyway, Dad had an alarm behind the cash register and he hit it, and one of the kids panicked and stabbed him. And that was it," Justin concluded.

"You mean he killed him?" Regina demanded.

Justin nodded, staring down into his glass. "Yup. After that everything fell apart fast. My mother started taking pills the doctors gave her to calm her down, and she's been taking them ever since. I took a year off from school to try to decide what to do about it all. I think the only thing that kept me from junking everything was Molly."

"Who's Molly?" Regina asked, taking a sip of Coke. She didn't know what to think of Justin's story. There was something so tough about the way he told it, but she could see sadness in his eyes the whole time he spoke. She thought that he was really suffering.

"Molly Hecht—do you know her? She's a senior— she and I were in the same class until I took time off. Blond, small . . . pretty," he added with a twisted smile.

Regina shook her head. "I don't think I know her," she said. "Is she your girlfriend?" Something about the way Justin said her name made Regina think he loved her.

He sighed. "Not now. She was, for years. Since junior high, if you can believe it. She really helped me through some tough times. Sometimes I think . . ." His voice trailed off as he stared over Regina's shoulder. "But anyway, that's history now," he said. "Molly's been in a lot of trouble lately. We're still really good friends, but I just can't be involved with her now. Not as long as she's involved with people like Jan Brown."

Regina wrinkled her nose. Those names sounded familiar, but she wasn't sure why. "Who's Jan Brown?"

"Part of the real hard-core drug set," Justin explained. "I love Molly, and I can't stand seeing her get mixed up with people like that. But there's only so much I can do." He looked sadly at Regina. "I think that's just about the worst part of growing up—admitting that sometimes you can't stop someone you love from growing away from you."

Regina was quiet for a minute. "Yeah," she said softly. "I know what you mean."

And she did too. Something in Justin's voice struck a chord in Regina, and she realized now what it was.

They were both lonely. But Justin's loneliness seemed so profound that it made Regina feel guilty about her own minor troubles. She wanted suddenly to help him. She wanted to make it up to him somehow—to show him that there was still such a thing in this world as loyalty and kindness.

Right then and there Regina vowed she was going to be a good friend to Justin Belson. And not just to take her mind off Bruce, though that was part of her motivation. It was going to be a long, long time before she got over Bruce, and there was no point pretending it was going to be easy.

The real reason was that she wanted to prove—to herself as well as to Justin—that she could make a difference to someone. She sure hadn't managed to make a difference to Bruce.

This time, though, it was going to be different. She would make sure of that.

Six

"**I** just want you to know, Jessica Wakefield, that your barbecue was one of the most perfect evenings of my entire life!" Amy hurried over to set her tray down next to Jessica's. A triumphant smile was on her face. It was Monday at noon, and the cafeteria was already crowded. But Amy seemed oblivious. She had one thing on her mind, and that was her own romantic situation—always a favorite topic of hers, but now that Bruce was in the picture, her sole subject of conversation.

Jessica put down the latest issue of *Glamour*, which she had been perusing while she waited for her friend. "I'm glad you had fun," she said dryly. "I don't suppose you care that my twin sister holds me responsible—or at least partly responsible—for wrecking her friendship with Regina?"

Amy poured dressing over her salad, completely unconcerned. "I'm sure Regina will forget all about their little tiff in a day or two," she said cheerfully. "Although," she added, dropping her voice, "I'm not really in any mood to encourage her to forgive Bruce. I have to ask your advice about this, Jess, because—" She floundered, unable to come up with anything more plausible than simply wanting to talk about herself—and Bruce. She tried another tack. "I mean, I hate to seem like the jealous type—at least at *this* stage. I mean before it's gotten really serious and everything. But I really do think that Bruce should forget all about Regina. It kind of gives me the creeps the way he keeps bringing up her name all the time. I mean it seems to me that Regina is *history* as far as he's concerned, don't you agree?"

Jessica ate a french fry, pretending to think it over. The truth was that Amy Sutton was beginning to turn into a real bore as far as Jessica was concerned. "You know," she said suddenly, leaning forward as she caught sight of Regina coming out of the lunch line, "I've seen Regina and Justin Belson together *three* times today, and it's only lunchtime. What do you think is going on between them?"

Amy narrowed her eyes. "Oh, Lord," she said, putting her fork down. "I hope Regina doesn't do something stupid like go rushing right into another relationship. It might make Bruce crazy."

Jessica ate another french fry. She didn't feel like reminding Amy of the obvious—that Bruce seemed to be rushing into a new relationship as well. Or at least Amy clearly hoped he was.

Actually, Jessica could see why Regina might find Justin appealing. He was definitely cute. Tall and angular, with moody, slightly romantic eyes, Justin always seemed to look as if he were ready to take on the world, whatever the cost.

With great interest, Jessica watched Justin and Regina head for a secluded table out on the sunlit patio. "They really don't seem to have much in common," she mused aloud. "Regina's got absolutely everything going for her, right? Straight A's, a good family, tons of money, incredible beauty—"

"Please," Amy said, an annoyed look on her face.

"Sorry." Jessica giggled. "I didn't mean to pump up the competition, but it's true." She looked thoughtfully at Justin, who was gesturing as he spoke. "And what's Justin got? He's on academic probation. He hangs out with a rough crowd. He's cute, but not gorgeous. I just don't see why Regina's interested, unless . . ." She leaned forward again, her expression intense.

"Unless what?" Amy demanded.

"Unless," Jessica said slowly, "that what my sister suggested is true—that Regina is so upset at the world that she wants to get revenge somehow. And maybe Justin Belson is the best way she can find to show us all that she's different now—that the old Regina just doesn't wait anymore."

"Maybe," Amy said, losing interest. "Maybe she's just hanging out with him till someone better comes along."

Jessica shook her head. She didn't think Regina was that kind of girl. Regina wouldn't make a new friend unless he were going to matter somehow. The only question was whether or not she was doing the right thing, falling in with someone whose middle name seemed to be Trouble.

"Let me give you my history notes," Regina offered, handing Justin her notebook. "Honestly, Justin, it's no trouble. I can pick them up from you in study hall."

Justin shook his head, smiling at her. "You want to give me everything. You tried to pay for drinks last night," he reminded her. "You didn't think I'd be warm enough so you wanted to give me your dad's sweater when we got back to your house. Now you're worried I'm going to flunk out of school, so you want to give me your history notes. What next?"

Regina blushed. "You think I'm being too maternal," she accused.

Justin laughed. "Don't think I don't like it. It's been a long time since anyone's fussed over me this way." He frowned suddenly, and Regina thought that one of the most fascinating things about him was how rapidly he shifted from joking around to utter seriousness. It was like watching storm clouds pass quickly across the sun. "Most of the time I'm the one who has to take care of things," he added softly. "Like taking care of my mother. Or taking care of Molly. It's nice feeling like you're so pulled together. But I've had enough experience on that side to know what a drag it is to take care of someone, Regina. I don't want you to feel that way about me."

Regina blushed and lowered her eyes. She wished she knew exactly how he *did* want her to feel. She wished she knew how she felt as well. It was astonishing to her that she should enjoy Justin's company so much. They had spent hours the night before at Kelly's, and she'd wanted the evening to go on and on. In some ways this was because Justin seemed to her almost like a creature from another world. None of the experiences he described or the people he knew well made any sense to her. She could hardly fathom what it must've been like when his father was killed, but that was only the tip of the iceberg.

But it wasn't just the unusual tragedy that set Justin apart for Regina. The truth was, she'd led an extremely sheltered life. Regina's parents adored their only daughter, and in any circumstances would have fought hard to protect her from pain. But the fact that she was born handicapped—and the fact that her mother believed herself responsible for Regina's hearing defect, since she had taken diet pills during the early months of pregnancy—made her parents feel guilty, and thus even more protective than they might have been. Regina had always been "special," and people had always looked out for her. True, her parents' wealth couldn't always protect her from danger—as proved by the time she was kidnapped by one of her father's bitter former employees. But Regina had rarely had the chance to get to know people from backgrounds different from her own.

Bruce came from a family every bit as wealthy as the Morrows. She and Bruce had big allowances, access to their parents' credit cards, their own expensive cars to drive. They might have had different value systems—Bruce felt much more entitled to luxuries than Regina did, for example—but they really were alike. They even *looked* alike in a way, with their dark hair and blue eyes.

Whereas Justin . . . well, Justin definitely appealed to Regina, and she guessed that might have something to do with the fact that he seemed rebellious. He didn't care about conventions. He was on academic probation because school bored him so much that he just skipped. Regina couldn't help admiring that—she, who had studied hard every night of her life, always got good grades and would never in a million years miss a class without permission. She thought Justin was amazingly daring. When she compared him to Bruce, he seemed even more daring. What risks had Bruce ever taken? What hardships had he ever overcome? Bruce had had life handed to him on a silver platter, but Justin . . . Justin had *suffered*. Regina thought he was the most romantic guy she'd ever met—more like a character in a book than a real person.

He appealed to her, yes, but she wasn't sure in what way. On the one hand she could tell there was a slightly romantic quality to their friendship already. The way he looked at her . . . the slight teasing sound

58

in his voice when he talked to her ... But then he talked about Molly all the time too. They had broken up, but who could say for how long? And at the same time Regina was well aware how much her own thoughts were still preoccupied with Bruce. She had barely slept for the past few nights, thinking about him.

I'd better watch myself, Regina chided inwardly. *All I need is to fall in love on the rebound. Justin is nice enough, that's true. And he's certainly interesting—but I just met him. I need to take it slow.*

"Justin," a female voice interrupted Regina's thoughts. "I've been looking for you. Can I sit down?"

"Sure," Justin said. "Regina, this is Molly. Molly, Regina Morrow."

Regina sat up straight, looking curiously at the tiny blonde whose feathery hair framed a small, intense face and a pair of piercing green eyes. "Hi," Molly said flatly, sitting down between Regina and Justin. "Jan told me you were out here, but—" She glanced significantly at Regina. "I couldn't believe it. You're never around at lunchtime, Justin. What's the deal?"

Justin flushed, looking annoyed. "I'm keeping Regina company," he said quietly.

Regina felt uncomfortable. Something strange seemed to be going on between Justin and Molly, and she felt that she was interrupting—or in the way.

"I came over here because I wanted to tell you that we're on for Saturday night," Molly said suddenly. She had a funny way of talking that made it sound as if she were slightly angry—or maybe she *was* angry. She didn't look at Regina when she mentioned Saturday night.

"Molly's mom goes out of town every year around this time," Justin explained. "Her dad lives in San Francisco, and that means Molly and her little brother Ty have the place to themselves."

"Yeah, so we have a huge party," Molly said, looking Regina up and down as she spoke to her. "An anything-goes sort of party. And I think Buzz is going to show," she told Justin.

Justin frowned. "Molly, I don't think—"

"Don't *mother* me," Molly snapped. She turned back to Regina with a funny little smile on her face. "I bet you'd like Buzz," she said insincerely. "He's a real good friend of mine. I hope Justin brings you to the party so you can meet him."

Regina blushed. She'd never met anyone like Molly before. "Thanks," she said awkwardly. "It sounds like fun."

Molly laughed—an unpleasantly harsh laugh which gave Regina the creeps. "Yeah," she said, getting to her feet. "It ought to be fun. Last year we had the time of our lives."

Justin looked at Molly with an expression Regina couldn't quite place. A lot of emotions seemed to flicker across his face—compassion, fondness, annoyance, something like despair. "I'll definitely be there," he said in a low voice. "But I'm serious, Molly. Don't let Buzz show up."

60

Molly tossed her hair back. "The thing about Buzz," she said with a smile, "is that you never know." She turned back to Regina and this time gave her a real smile—one that lit her face up like an incandescent bulb and made her suddenly, and touchingly, beautiful. "Please come," she said gently, putting her hand on Regina's shoulder. "I don't even know who you are, but any friend of Justin's is a friend of mine. I mean it."

Regina stared after her as she hurried away. "Wow," she said at last. "So that's Molly."

Justin smiled. "Yeah, that's Molly," he said, shaking his head. He was watching her walk away too. Regina wished she could tell what he was thinking. But as she was beginning to realize, Justin Belson wasn't that easy to figure out.

And from the looks of it, neither was Molly Hecht.

Seven

With a frown Elizabeth took her history book from her locker. "I just don't get it," she said to Enid, who was standing beside her. "Regina and Bruce have only been broken up since Saturday. Today's Wednesday. In the space of four days she suddenly seems like a different person!"

"It happens," Enid said reasonably. "Remember, Liz, she's been through a real shock. Whatever she may have suspected about Bruce and Amy, she still didn't know their relationship was going to blow up in her face the way it did. You know what happens when people suffer terrible loss—they go to extremes."

"Well," Elizabeth said, slamming her locker door shut, "you can certainly say that Regina is going to extremes. She's with Justin and his friends every single time I see her!" Her blue-green eyes were filled with concern. "Look, I may end up messing things up again, but I want to let her know that I'm behind her.

I'm going to try to find her during study hall to tell her I'm sorry."

"Be careful," Enid advised. "Something tells me she's going to be more than a little touchy. Ken told me that Bruce said she pretends he doesn't exist. She hangs up when he calls her, won't say hello to him—she's really giving him the silent treatment."

Elizabeth sighed. "I don't really blame her," she confessed. "What Bruce and Amy did to her on Saturday night was unforgivable. And I'm afraid I really owe her an apology for my role in the whole mess. I just want to find her and let her know that's how I feel."

"Look, there she is right now," Enid exclaimed, pointing as Regina rounded a corner and passed through the main corridor with Justin.

"Wait here," Elizabeth urged her. "I'll just be a second." History book tucked under her arm, she hurried down the hallway after the couple.

"Regina!" she exclaimed when she was within earshot. "Can I talk to you for a second?"

Regina turned, her face completely impassive. "I guess so," she said flatly. "Liz, do you know Justin?"

"Nice to meet you," Elizabeth said.

Justin nodded at her. "You're the one with the twin sister, right?" he said.

Elizabeth nodded, wondering how she was going to be able to get Regina away from Justin long enough to talk to her.

But Regina solved the problem for her. "Justin, I'll

63

meet you after class," she murmured, patting his arm with her hand. "Are we still set for this afternoon?"

"Absolutely," Justin said, squeezing her arm affectionately. "See you later!" And with that he slipped away through the crowded hallway.

"Justin's taking me for a ride on his motorcycle after school," Regina announced. Her voice struck Elizabeth as more than a little defiant, and she remembered Jeffrey's warning about being careful.

"Well, I'm not the best person to talk about motorcycles," Elizabeth said, trying to keep her voice light. Elizabeth had almost been killed some months earlier when her former boyfriend, Todd Wilkins, had taken her for a ride on his motorcycle and they'd gotten in a terrible accident. She had been in a coma for days and had suffered temporary changes in her personality which still frightened her when she thought of them. The Morrows hadn't moved to Sweet Valley when her accident occurred, but Elizabeth had told Regina all about it some time ago.

"I think it'll be fun," Regina said defensively. "That's what I like about Justin," she added. "He isn't afraid of anything. He really takes control of things."

Elizabeth didn't respond. She couldn't help thinking that from everything she'd heard about Justin, this was only part of the story. How much control could he be taking if he was almost flunking out of school? "He seems nice," she said cautiously. "But, Regina, I've heard some scary things about a few of his friends. That girl Jan Brown, and her boyfriend, Jay Benson

. . . some of those kids are heavily into drugs. And not just marijuana either."

"Liz, I don't need you to lecture me about Justin's friends," Regina snapped, her mouth a tight line. "You don't even know what you're talking about!"

Elizabeth felt her heart beating faster. "I'm sorry," she said quickly. "Regina, the reason I wanted to talk to you was because I felt so bad about Saturday night, and—"

"I never want to talk about Saturday night again," Regina cried, her lips trembling. "Look," she added, fighting for control, "what's done is done, OK? Bruce and Amy seem perfectly happy together, and I'm glad for them. The truth is that Bruce and I didn't have very much in common anyway. I'm better off without him."

"But I don't want you to feel that our friendship is a thing of the past too," Elizabeth said passionately. "Regina, I feel awful about my role in that whole disaster. I want you to know—"

Regina cut her off again. "I just don't want to talk about it," she said stubbornly.

"At least watch out for yourself," Elizabeth begged, trying another tack. "I can see how you'd feel like you want to get away from all your old friends and everything, but you've got to promise to be careful. Some of Justin's friends—"

Regina began to tremble with rage. "Stop it, Liz," she cried, her face dead white. "I don't want your advice, OK? I want you to leave me alone. And for your information, Justin and his friends are a whole lot better for me than you and *your* friends. So why don't you just butt out and leave me alone!" And with that she spun on her heel and raced off, leaving Elizabeth staring after her with her mouth open.

"Well?" Enid said curiously when she returned to her locker.

Elizabeth shook her head, her eyes filling with tears. "I guess I wasn't careful enough," she said sadly.

Enid frowned. "I hope Regina can handle Justin," she murmured. "I remember how hard it was for *me* to handle the fast crowd." Enid had been mixed up with the wrong set for a while when she was much younger, and had been through some hard times before she realized how dangerous they were for her.

Elizabeth nodded emphatically. Instead of making amends with Regina, she had alienated the girl completely.

Amy and Bruce were supposed to meet Amy's cousin Mimi in town at the Box Tree Café after school on Thursday. This meeting, which had been scheduled and postponed at least three times already, was supposed to be their opportunity for some real inside information on drug sources in the area, and they were hoping Mimi would tell them things that would make their report more revealing.

Mimi's knowledge about the drug scene was fairly extensive. At nineteen Mimi was a junior at Sweet Valley College, studying to be a social worker. She had been working part time at a clinic outside of town for the past four years, and had learned a lot about drug abuse and rehabilitation. Her job gave her the authorized story on the drug situation, but she also knew enough people both at college and in the community to know the underground scene as well.

To their delight, Amy and Bruce found that Mimi really was a gold mine of information. They fired questions at her for half an hour or so and had barely exhausted their list when she turned the conversation to what seemed to be an entirely different subject.

"Do either of you two know a senior named Margaret Hecht?" Mimi asked, dropping her voice.

"Margaret Hecht?" Bruce repeated slowly. "I don't think so. Why?"

"She's supposedly part of a group of kids at Sweet Valley High who are really heavily into drugs. I've got a few other names—Janice Brown, James Benson . . . but the reason I'm bringing up Margaret's name is that she's supposed to have a big open party at her mother's house on Saturday night, and it looks like one of the biggest dealers in my college is number one on her guest list."

"Margaret . . . you mean Molly!" Bruce exclaimed. "Oh, God—that's Justin Belson's old girlfriend," he exclaimed to Amy. "The guy Regina's been hanging around with."

"So you know Molly Hecht?" Mimi pressed.

Bruce nodded. "At least by sight, anyway. She's a tiny little blonde."

"Well, from the people I've talked to, she isn't the problem—it's her best friend Jan who is. This girl Janice Brown seems to be incredibly messed up. I don't know how they ever got to know Buzz Jackson, but for their sake they'd be better off without him."

"Wait, wait," Amy begged, scribbling frantically. "Who is Buzz Jackson?"

"Buzz," Mimi said portentiously, "happens to be the biggest cocaine dealer at my college right now. He's bad news," she added, "and there just isn't that much more to say about him. He's my age—maybe a year older. A skinny, sort of mean-looking guy who's been dealing drugs since junior high." Mimi laughed bitterly. "Let's just say that now it's a full-time occupation. Buzz latches on to people like Jan and Molly—basically OK kids who have the cash or can get the cash somehow—to become steady customers. It's almost entirely cocaine now, though knowing Buzz, it could be anything." She grimaced. "See, that's the whole problem. When you buy drugs, you have no idea what you're getting. Guys like Buzz are worried about one thing—getting rid of the stuff they have as fast as possible."

"Is this guy's name really Buzz?" Bruce demanded.

Mimi shrugged. "I think he's got some first name that he hates, like William. Buzz is a nickname—you can probably guess where he got it. Look, the reason I'm telling you guys this is that you can do me a favor—in exchange for all the stuff I told you about the clinic."

68

"We'll be happy to, Mimi," Amy promised.

"'We're trying hard to get Buzz locked up," Mimi confided. "The people I work for at the clinic really want him put away. We've been working with private detectives for the past month trying to track him down—that's how I know he's been invited to the Hechts' on Saturday."

"What can we do to help?" Bruce demanded.

"Well," Mimi replied, "if you know anyone who's supposed to go to the party, warn them. Buzz is a smooth operator, and he's been known to get kids who have never so much as tasted a sip of beer to try something dangerous."

Bruce paled. "I better call Regina," he muttered. Amy looked away, clearly unenthusiastic about the prospect, but aware it would hardly make her look good if she objected.

"Mimi, thanks so much," Amy said a minute later as she and Bruce prepared to leave. She patted her cousin on the arm. "You've been incredibly helpful."

"Don't even think about it," Mimi said, smiling at her.

Bruce didn't say anything. He was thinking about Regina.

On Thursday evening Regina was up in her bedroom, looking absently at a set of equations she was supposed to balance for chemistry class. Her mind wasn't on her homework, though. She kept thinking about Justin Belson. It seemed incredible to her that she had known him less than a week and he already occupied her thoughts so completely. She wasn't even certain that she was interested in him in a romantic way—certainly not in the way she'd experienced previously. When she thought about Justin, she felt an overwhelming desire to protect him. Right now, for instance, she wondered if he was alone at his house—if his mother had been too doped-up with pills to make him dinner . . . if he'd even started looking at his homework. She was just trying to decide whether or not to call and ask him if he wanted help with his homework when Nicholas knocked on the door to her bedroom. "Telephone," he said. "I think it's Bruce."

Regina frowned. "I told you—I don't want to talk to him," she said.

"Tell him yourself," Nicholas said. "I'm not going to keep screening your calls for you, Regina. Anyway, don't you think it's time you two straightened this out for yourselves?"

Regina glared at him, picking up the receiver next to her desk. "Hello," she said coldly.

"Regina? It's Bruce. And look—don't hang up," he pleaded. "I know how mad you are at me and I don't blame you. I acted like a total jerk on Saturday night."

Regina listened in frozen silence.

"I need to see you," Bruce said. "I can't explain all this over the phone. Regina, I really want to be your friend. I can't bear the thought of us ending up hating each other, like—"

"Please," Regina said icily. "Spare me, Bruce. I

don't need to hear this kind of soap opera stuff."

"Fine," Bruce said, sighing heavily. "Forget it, then. But there's another reason I'm calling. This guy Justin Belson—how much do you know about him?"

"Enough," Regina snapped. "But then how much does anyone ever know someone else? I thought I knew *you*, and I'd never have guessed in a million years you'd treat me the way you did on Saturday night."

Bruce was quiet for a minute. "OK," he said, obviously stung. "Touché, Regina."

"Is that all? I've got a lot of homework to do."

"No," Bruce said, "that isn't *all*. There's supposed to be some big party at this girl Molly Hecht's place on Saturday. I assume Justin is going, since he and Molly used to be close. I'm calling to warn you, Regina. Amy's cousin Mimi told us that one of the biggest drug dealers in the area is supposed to show up there. I don't want you to get hurt."

"Tell *Amy*," Regina said in a scathing voice, "that I very much appreciate her concern—*and* her cousin's. The fact is, I can take care of myself."

Bruce didn't answer, and a moment later Regina hung up, not bothering to say good-bye. It was only then that she realized she was trembling with anger.

How dare Bruce call up and act as if he had the right to protect her from getting hurt? He was the one who had hurt her in the first place. She was never going to forgive him for that—never. And she certainly wasn't going to listen to his ridiculous advice!

Eight

"Jessica, I can't believe you waited until now to tell me about this!" Elizabeth wailed. "Amy told you all this stuff Thursday night about Molly's party?"

Jessica pretended to concentrate on filing her nails with an emery board. The twins had been dawdling over Saturday morning breakfast when Jessica dropped the bombshell. From the expression on her twin's face, it was clear that a crisis was in the offing.

"I just didn't think it was something Regina couldn't handle, that's all." Jessica sniffed. "Anyway, you always get mad at me when I spread rumors."

"It figures," Elizabeth said, shaking her head. "The one time I would've liked to have a little advance warning about something, you decide to get coy about 'spreading rumors.'" She jumped up from the table, clearly distraught.

"Where are you going?" Jessica demanded.

"To call Regina, of course," Elizabeth yelled behind

her as she hurried upstairs. She could barely think straight. Some drug dealer named Buzz was going to show up at Molly's party! She couldn't believe it. She just had to convince Regina not to go. Elizabeth dialed the Morrows' phone number with trembling fingers, hoping against hope that Regina had forgiven her by now and would be willing to listen.

"Regina? It's Elizabeth Wakefield," she said anxiously after Regina picked up the phone.

"Oh . . . hi," Regina said. It was hard to tell from the tone of her voice what she was thinking, so Elizabeth decided to plunge bravely ahead.

"Regina, I wanted to apologize again for our misunderstanding," she began.

"Oh, don't worry about it," Regina said. "I've been in such a weird mood all week, and I'm sure I jumped at you the other day at school. I didn't mean—"

"I'm so glad you're not mad at me anymore!" Elizabeth cut in, overjoyed. "That means you won't get mad when I tell you what Jessica just told me about Molly Hecht's party."

An icy silence followed, but Elizabeth—heartened by Regina's initial warmth—just kept on talking. "The thing is, Regina, I'm sure Justin's a nice guy, but what do you really know about Molly? Or Jan Brown? Or any of their friends? Apparently some guy named Buzz is supposed to show up at the Hechts' house—with drugs. Real drugs—stuff like cocaine and speed."

Regina's voice was extremely cold. "Thank you, Liz. But if you called to warn me about Justin—*or* Molly—

73

let me assure you that I can take care of myself. It's nice of you to be concerned," she added stiffly. "But I really don't think it's necessary."

Elizabeth stared blankly down at the floor. Now what? Clearly she had put her foot in her mouth—again. "Well . . . I guess you know Justin better than I do," she managed weakly.

"Yes," Regina said. "I do, Liz."

Elizabeth cleared her throat. "Just promise me you'll be careful," she begged.

Regina paused for a second. "Thanks for calling," she said flatly. And with that she hung up, leaving Elizabeth feeling completely helpless.

Regina stared at herself in the full-length mirror in her bedroom closet, her blue eyes slightly absentminded as she buttoned up her cardigan sweater. She wasn't really sure what everyone else would be wearing to Molly's party. Some of Justin's friends dressed strangely; Regina would probably stand out in her conservative gray flannel pants and sweater. But she couldn't really concentrate on her outfit anyway. She felt terrible. She'd barely gotten any sleep for the past few nights, and she could see puffy circles under her eyes. For the first time since the previous Saturday night, when this whole dreadful mess had begun, Regina allowed herself to admit the magnitude of what had happened.

She couldn't believe how alienated she felt from her friends—from her old way of life. It wasn't just Bruce.

And it wasn't just Elizabeth either—though Regina's phone conversation with Elizabeth had pained her terribly. Even her relationship with her family had changed. Nicholas was furious with her for going out with Justin again that night, and hadn't spoken to her all day. And her parents were being stricter than usual, probably due to Nicholas's influence, insisting she come home by midnight.

All her life Regina had been obedient and respectful. It shocked her to realize how quickly she had fallen into Justin's way of thinking and seeing things. According to Justin, authority—no matter what kind— was bad. If someone told you not to do something, chances were you should go ahead and do it—if only to show them how stupid rules were in the first place. Regina had admired Justin for that very bravado, but now . . . well, she was confused. Very confused. She had mixed feelings about the party at Molly's house, and though she hadn't yet admitted it to Justin, she wasn't sure she really wanted to go.

And she'd been terrible to Elizabeth on the phone. Of course her friend had called to warn her! Wouldn't Regina have done the same thing if the situation were reversed? But instead of understanding Elizabeth's position and listening to her, she had become short-tempered and defensive.

She didn't even blame Elizabeth or Nicholas—or even Bruce—for trying to warn her about the party. She kept remembering the look Molly had given her earlier that week when she told her about Buzz. *Buzz.*

Just the name gave Regina the creeps.

Well, the one thing to do was to tell Justin her fears. He would understand. The good thing about Justin was that she could tell him anything.

But before she met Justin there was something she had to do. Without a moment's hesitation she crossed the room, opened the desk drawer, and pulled out a pad of paper. For the next few minutes she was busy writing. It took several drafts before she had the letter the way she wanted it. Then she folded it, put it in an envelope, and addressed it carefully. She would drop it in a mailbox on her way out to meet Justin.

In fact, Regina felt better just having written it. The letter was the first step. The next was to talk to Justin.

"I don't think you have anything to worry about," Justin said affectionately, patting Regina on the shoulder. They had stopped at Casey's Place for a soda before heading over to Molly's place, and Regina had been filling Justin in on her anxieties about Buzz. "I mean, look—what's the very worst that can happen? Say Buzz does show up, which I don't think is very likely anyway. All you've got to do is just ignore the guy." Justin frowned, slumping down in the booth and making wet circles on the table with his glass. "*I'm* worried about Molly," he added. "It seems to me that the worst thing that can happen is just more of the same. Which is that either Buzz will show up or he won't, but in any case Molly will get really high and do something stupid—as usual."

Regina frowned. "I don't want to sound like a baby, but I'm not sure it's such a good idea, heading over there when we know there could be trouble." She looked earnestly at Justin. "Don't you want to get off probation and start applying yourself? You're so smart, Justin. If you really put your mind to it—"

Justin flinched. "Please," he said. "No lectures. I get enough of that from the social workers they make me talk to—I don't need it from you too."

Regina looked hurt. "Is that what you think of me as—another social worker type?"

"Well, sometimes you act like it," Justin said with a sigh. The next instant he looked apologetic. "I'm sorry, Regina," he amended. "I don't mean to sound like this. I'm worried about Molly and I'm taking it out on you."

Regina looked around the crowded ice cream parlor, suppressing the question that had been on her lips almost every minute that she spent with Justin. What was it about his relationship with Molly? On the one hand he insisted that they had broken up. But Regina got the distinct impression there was more to it than that. The look on Justin's face when he said Molly's name . . . the amount of concern he felt for her . . . He was still in love with her, Regina decided. And it was a good thing she'd realized it soon enough to keep herself from getting terribly hurt. Because however friendly Justin had been to her, he'd never given her the slightest reason to believe he had any romantic interest in her. He never tried to kiss her or hold her hand. In fact, most of the time his behavior was more fraternal than anything else.

Justin seemed to be reading her mind. "You're wondering about 'us,' aren't you," he said softly. "You have that look on your face that you get sometimes . . . like I'm a puzzle or a math problem or something and you're trying to figure me out."

Regina stared at her hands. "That's not very flattering. I hate to think I treat people like math problems. But you're right if you think I'm confused about you, Justin. I can't help wondering about your feelings for Molly."

Justin stared at her. "What does Molly have to do with anything?" he demanded, looking as though she'd wounded him.

"I think she has a lot to do with everything," Regina persevered. "If you want my honest opinion, Justin, I think it's stupid to decide you're going to break up with someone just because she's in trouble. Not if you still love her, that is. Shouldn't you just throw yourself in there and fight—and make sure you keep her out of danger?"

Justin paled. Clearly Regina had hit a nerve. "I don't know what you mean," he said slowly.

"Justin, it's obvious how much you still care about her," Regina said. "Why try to hide it? It's only going to make you miserable to watch her from the sidelines."

Justin fidgeted for a moment before speaking. "You know, you're an amazing girl, Regina," he said at last.

"For some reason I feel like I can really talk to you. I know we've only known each other for a short time, but I already feel there are things I can tell you that I can't tell anyone else. Does that sound crazy to you?"

Regina shook her head. "Not at all," she murmured. "I feel really close to you, too, Justin."

"Well, the funny thing is that if you'd told me a week ago that we'd be sitting here having this conversation, I would've laughed my head off. I mean, I've looked up to you, Regina. Don't laugh, because it's true. It seemed to me like you had it all together. Looks, money, friends, good grades. And it wasn't like you hadn't had to fight for things. You had that handicap to overcome, and you did it. I thought you were a hero. I really have always thought so." He looked agitated. "I guess I had a crush on you more than anything else. After Molly . . ." He paused and shook his head. "Well, you're right. I love Molly, and I guess deep down I always will. But I'm trying to get out of that whole thing because I felt like she was dragging me down so much. I want things to be good again, you know?"

Regina nodded. "I know," she said simply. "But I also know what it's like from Molly's angle. I know what it's like to be involved with someone when things are falling apart, and to have that person just take off and find someone new without trying to fight for the relationship. Justin, I think you owe it to Molly to try. Just to *try*. Because I'm not convinced you're over it yet, and until you are, you and I don't have a chance."

Justin was quiet then for a long time. When he looked up, his eyes were shining with tears. "You're a good friend, Regina Morrow," he said softly.

And when he smiled at her, Regina had the sense that there was something really special about Justin Belson. Something no one had ever recognized before.

She was really glad they were friends.

Nine

"I don't think I can stand it," Elizabeth muttered. It was early Saturday evening and she was pacing back and forth in her bedroom. It was almost seven o'clock, and in about fifteen minutes Jeffrey was supposed to come by to pick the twins up—they had been invited over to the Fowlers' estate to watch rented movies on Mr. Fowler's full-sized screen along with Bruce, Amy, Ken Matthews, Cara Walker, and Enid. But Elizabeth couldn't keep her mind on the plans for the evening. All she could think about was Regina, Molly's party, and the horrible-sounding Buzz.

"What am I supposed to do?" she wailed to Jessica, who was in the bathroom that connected the twins' rooms, blithely trying on spray on hair color. "I just can't let Regina go over to the Hechts'. I can't!"

"I hate to say it, but I don't really see how much choice you have," Jessica pointed out. "Look, this stuff goes on just like spray paint," she added, admiring the reddish streaks she'd applied. "Isn't it fun? I look like a rock star."

"You look like a freak," Elizabeth said gloomily. "Help me, Jess! Tell me what I should do."

"Well, you could call Nicholas," Jessica offered. "That way at least you'd dump some of the responsibility on to *him*."

Elizabeth's eyes widened. "That's not such a bad idea," she admitted. "You know, Jess, you may have a point. Why didn't I think of it myself?"

"Thanks," Jessica said dryly, reaching for her makeup kit. "Isn't it possible for me to come up with something original—just once?"

"Nicholas," Elizabeth mused. She and Nicholas had always liked each other, and for a brief time had confused mutual attraction for something much more important. But now all that was in the past. Nicholas had become a good friend to Elizabeth, and she knew she could speak openly to him about her worries.

Jessica's notion of "dumping responsibility" was all wrong as far as Elizabeth was concerned. But by telling Nicholas, she could at least sound out his advice on how to proceed. It seemed to her that keeping quiet about Molly's party would be impossible. Hadn't she decided to keep quiet last week—with terrible results?

No, it was definitely up to her to say something this time. And Jessica was right about Nicholas. Her spirits lifted, Elizabeth hastened to the phone. It was several minutes after Nola answered that Nicholas picked up the receiver. Elizabeth tried in the meantime to decide the best way to tell him what she knew. In the end she put things plainly and simply.

"Nicholas, it's Liz Wakefield," she said rapidly. "I hate to bug you, but I'm kind of worried about Regina, and I thought I'd ask you what you think I should do."

"You're not the only one who's worried," Nicholas said firmly. "What's up, Liz?"

"Well, it's this party tonight over at Molly Hecht's," Elizabeth began. Soon she had filled Nicholas in on everything she knew—the rumor floating around that there would be drugs at the party and that a notorious dealer named Buzz might show up. "I didn't feel right about calling you at first, but when I tried to talk about it with Regina, she wouldn't listen to me," Elizabeth explained.

Nicholas was quiet for a while. "I can't even believe it," he said raggedly. "Regina's going to a party where there will be drugs?" His voice broke. "Liz, thanks for telling me. Now, tell me again the name of this girl who's throwing the party."

"Molly Hecht. I don't know her exact address, but I think her house is on Los Brisos Drive."

"Got it," Nicholas said in a tight voice. "OK, Liz. And thanks. You have no idea how glad I am that you called me."

"What are you going to do?" Elizabeth demanded.

"I'm going over there," Nicholas said grimly. "And I'm going to bring Regina home and try to talk some sense into her."

Elizabeth sighed heavily. She knew Regina would be furious with her. But she felt she'd done the right thing nonetheless.

She just hoped Nicholas got to the party before anything awful had happened.

It took Nicholas a lot longer than he'd planned to get on his way to look for Regina. First he couldn't find the keys to his Jeep. Then he couldn't find his wallet. His parents were out and neither Nola or any of the other servants had any idea where it was. Finally, despairing, he ran out of the house with the keys, deciding he'd just have to drive without his wallet, which had his license inside.

It seemed as if everything were destined to go wrong. He couldn't find Los Brisos Drive on the index of his map of Sweet Valley, and after driving aimlessly for about fifteen minutes, he decided he'd have to come up with a better plan. He finally drove into a gas station and looked Molly's address up in a phone book. By then it was eight o'clock and his hands were sweating. Nicholas didn't know why, but he had a terrible feeling in his chest and head. He felt as if he were suffocating with tension. The sooner he saw Regina, the better.

He was so worried that he didn't even realize he was exceeding the speed limit by ten miles an hour—not until he heard the siren and saw the squad car's red flashing lights in his rearview mirror. "Darn," he muttered, staring helplessly down at the empty spot on the seat beside him where his wallet usually lay.

"Son, do you realize this is a twenty-five-mile-per-hour zone?" the police officer asked, sticking his head inside the window when Nicholas had pulled the Jeep over.

Nicholas bit his lip. He knew what was coming. "Look, sir, I'm terribly sorry, but I'm in trouble," he blurted out. "I think my sister may be in some kind of an emergency and I—"

"Son," the officer interrupted, "nine times out of ten when we stop people they tell us they were going somewhere in a hurry. Can I see your license, please?"

Nicholas stared helplessly at the clock before him. It was almost eight-fifteen. "I . . . uh, look, I know this sounds crazy, but—"

"I know," the officer said ironically, rocking back and forth as he looked Nicholas over. "Too rushed to bring it along with you, right?"

Nicholas gulped. "Please," he begged. "I think my sister may be in real danger and I—"

"Why don't you come down to the station with us," the officer suggested, opening the door to the Jeep. "I don't see any reason why we can't talk this whole thing over. But this isn't the place to do it."

Nicholas threw up his hands. There was nothing he could do but get out of the Jeep and follow the policeman to the squad car.

He just had to hope he could explain things fast enough to get a squad car sent out to the Hechts' place. Regina might never forgive him, but it was a chance he was going to have to take.

Regina looked around her, trying hard not to show

how shocked she was by the scene greeting her eyes inside the Hechts' modern ranch house on Los Brisos Drive. The house was almost entirely dark. Candles were lit in the living room and the stereo was playing so loud it was hard to hear anything. The place was packed—mostly with people Regina had never seen before. Some of them were apparently friends of Ty's, Molly's ninth-grade brother. Others looked older, like college kids. The house smelled like beer and cigarette smoke, and Regina felt slightly queasy as someone— she didn't recognize her—handed her a beer.

"Justin," she said uneasily, "don't you think—"

"Don't worry," Justin said reassuringly, squeezing her arm. "Look, there's Molly."

Sure enough, Molly was winding her way through the dark, crowded living room, a funny expression on her face. "Hey," she said, giving Justin a kiss that seemed to Regina to be more than just friendly. She stared at Regina as if she didn't recognize her, and her expression was anything but welcoming. Regina remembered how she'd felt the week before when she saw Bruce and Amy together. She wanted to assure Molly that she and Justin were just friends, but how could she? Even if they were alone, the music was so loud she could barely hear herself think. Feeling awkward and shy, Regina took a sip of the beer she'd been given. It tasted sour and slightly strange, but not unpleasant. She took another sip and tried to relax. Something told her it was going to be a long evening.

"So *you're* the rich girl we've been hearing so much

about," a sharp voice said suddenly.

Regina whirled about to face a tall, mean-looking girl whose arms were folded across her chest. "I'm Jan Brown," the girl added, as if Regina should know who she was. "I heard you didn't even *drink*," she added accusingly, staring at the beer can in Regina's hand. "I heard all you did was sit around and *study*."

Regina felt miserable. "How do you know who I am? I don't know who *you* are," she said.

Jan shrugged. By now Justin and Molly were dancing, and Regina could see no escape from this unpleasant conversation. "We know all about you," Jan said in a sinister voice. "My boyfriend Jay and I have been doing—what do you call it—a little *research* on you. Soon as we found out Justin was hanging around with you. Has he hit you up for a loan yet? I hear your dad's loaded."

Regina's eyes filled with tears, but she blinked them away, determined not to let Jan see how disturbed she was. She took a big gulp of beer, wishing she hadn't come. "Justin and I are just friends," she said, somewhat pointlessly. "I know how much he still cares for Molly."

Jan's eyes narrowed. "That's really considerate of you," she said sarcastically. "I'm sure Molly will be touched." She lit a cigarette, and Regina couldn't help thinking that she looked incredibly hard and used up, though she couldn't be older than seventeen.

"This party is going to be wild," Jan said, changing the subject. "I bet you have the time of your life." She winked, and Regina shifted uncomfortably. She felt a little light-headed, either from the beer or from the close, smoky room. "You do drugs?" Jan asked, exhaling smoke through her nose.

Regina shook her head.

"Aw," Jan said, pouting, "why not? I thought rich kids like you were the ones who knew how to have fun."

"I just never wanted to," Regina said, feeling like an idiot. She wished Justin would come back from dancing with Molly. She was getting sick of Jan.

"Well, tonight may just be your lucky night," Jan said softly. "Did Justin tell you Buzz is dropping in?"

Regina shivered. She hated the look on Jan's face. To her immense relief she saw Molly and Justin coming toward them. From their expressions it appeared as if they'd been having an argument—though how they could hear each other with so much racket from the stereo, Regina couldn't tell.

"I told you I want you to cut it out, and I mean cut it out!" she heard Justin say in a tense voice.

Molly looked close to tears. "I can't help it. I just can't," she said. At first Regina thought Justin would relent, but he turned away, his face impassive, and came back over to Regina. "Let's dance," he said, pulling her hand.

Jan gave them both a scathing look. "You two look real sweet together, Justin. Like two kids at the prom," she said in a nasty voice.

Regina felt a chill go down her back. "Jan really

gives me the creeps," she told Justin when they were out of earshot.

"Don't mind her," Justin said loudly, over the pulsing music. "She's crazy, that's all."

Regina wished she found this comforting. She was about to ask Justin how much longer he wanted to stay when the doorbell rang. No one seemed to hear at first because of the stereo, but eventually Molly went to the front door and came back a few minutes later, dragging a thin, scraggly guy behind her. She had a big smirk on her face.

"Shut up! Everyone shut up!" she squealed. "It's Buzz!"

Someone turned the stereo down, though Regina still thought it was too loud to bear. Buzz didn't seem to mind, though. He spread his arms out, and with a terrible grin hollered, "OK, everyone, let's party!"

Regina shivered. The guy gave her the creeps. And she didn't like the glazed expressions on the rapt faces around her. She wanted to go home. And the sooner they left, the better.

Ten

"OK, son," the police officer said, putting his hands in his pockets and staring hard at Nicholas. "Let me see if I've got this straight. You say your sister is at a party tonight where you suspect that the guests may be using illegal drugs. Am I right?"

"Yes," Nicholas said, running his hands through his dark hair. "You're right."

Nicholas was seated on a bench in the front room of the Sweet Valley Police Department while Sergeant O'Riley asked him questions. He knew he was at fault for driving without his license, but he just wished they would hurry up and get over to the Hechts' place. He couldn't bear the thought of Regina surrounded by those creepy kids. The minutes were flying past too—it was almost nine o'clock.

"Listen, Jim," Sergeant Henderson said, coming out of his office with a frown, "I think we'd better do a check on the place, just to be sure. You say it's on Los Brisos Drive?"

Nicholas nodded. "I wouldn't have said anything about drugs if I didn't have a good reason to be scared," he said seriously. "I don't want to get anyone in trouble, but I'm worried about my sister."

"I don't blame you, son." Sergeant O'Riley patted him on the shoulder. "Look, we're going to have to give you a ticket for exceeding the speed limit and driving without your license. But we can write it up later. Right now I think it's more important that we get over to this place on Los Brisos and see what's going on over there."

Nicholas jumped to his feet. "Thank you," he said gratefully. His heart was pounding.

He couldn't have borne to sit there for another minute. It felt as if it were taking forever to get to the Hechts' place so he could make sure Regina was all right.

Regina looked around Molly's living room in confusion. Where was Justin? She didn't want to admit it, but she was definitely feeling the effects of the beer she had drunk. She felt wobbly and light-headed, and wanted to get her coat and go outside for some fresh air. She scanned the room for Justin, so she could tell him what she was going to do, but he seemed to be nowhere in sight. After searching several minutes she gave up and headed for the bedroom where she knew Molly had put the coats. The door was closed, and no one answered when she knocked. "Can I come in?" she said, pushing it open.

"Well, would you look who's here," Jan drawled. She and Molly were sitting cross-legged on the floor, a red-haired girl named Tina with them. The room was filled with marijuana smoke, and Regina drew back, coughing.

"What's the matter? Haven't you ever smelled dope before?" Jan demanded with a smirk.

Regina blushed. "Of course I have," she said. She knew it was stupid to let them make her feel like a baby, but she couldn't help it. Molly inhaled deeply from the thin cigarette, her eyes half closed, and passed it to Tina while Jan looked on.

"Why don't you join us?" Jan drawled. "Or are you too busy stealing Molly's boyfriend away from her?"

Regina flinched, staring at Molly. The blonde looked pale and her eyes were puffy. Had she been crying? Suddenly Regina felt terrible. She remembered the events of the previous weekend with agony. Had she made Molly suffer as much tonight as Amy had made *her* suffer last Saturday?

"I'm not stealing Justin," Regina said awkwardly. "We're just friends, Molly. He still loves you."

Molly looked at her woodenly. Only the expression in her eyes revealed the pain she was experiencing.

"Come off it, Regina," Jan scoffed, taking the cigarette from Tina and inhaling expertly. "We all know what you're like," she added when she had breathed in the smoke. "Miss Goody-Two-Shoes came down for a night to watch the freaks, right? Only you plan to take a souvenir with you when you leave the zoo—Justin."

"I don't know what you're talking about," Regina said, her lips clenched. "I only came tonight because—"

"Because of Justin," Jan filled in for her in a mocking voice. "Sure, Regina. We understand. You didn't have anything else to do so you decided to hang out with the freaks and steal Molly's boyfriend."

Regina was starting to get angry. "Look," she said. "I came tonight because Justin invited me, but I have no intention of stealing him from anyone. Besides, Justin isn't an object. He's a person. If everything were absolutely perfect between Molly and him, I wouldn't be here tonight. But that's not my fault." She paused. *Any more than it was really Amy's fault that Bruce fell for her,* she admitted painfully. *The truth was that he and I drifted apart. If it hadn't been Amy, it would've been someone else.*

Molly was staring at her, her eyes wide. Regina wasn't sure why, but something in her face made her feel as if they could be friends. Jan was the impossible one, not Molly. But Molly seemed to be afraid of Jan. When Jan spoke, Molly just sat back and listened.

"Hey, you guys!" Ty Hecht shrieked, barging into the bedroom. "Buzz is getting out the stuff right now, and he told me to tell you to hurry before it's all gone."

Regina grabbed onto the molding of the doorway to steady herself. Tina and Molly were jumping up,

93

and Jan was already halfway out the door.

This looked like as good a time as any to grab her coat and sneak away. Regina had had it with these people. She wasn't even going to try to find Justin to say good night. All she wanted was to get outside and clear her head.

"Hey," Jan called from the spot on the living room floor where she was sitting with a group around Buzz. "Where are you sneaking off to, Regina? The party's just getting started."

Regina practically jumped. She hadn't expected anyone would notice her, especially since the music had been turned back up to a ridiculous level. "I'm just going out for a walk," she mumbled.

Justin was sitting next to Molly, apparently arguing with her. When he looked up to see Regina walking away, he suddenly seemed to realize he'd been neglecting her. He jumped up and put his hand on her arm. "Come sit down for a little while. Then I'll take a walk with you," he said, looking concerned.

Jan gave Regina a dirty look. "We're having a perfectly good time right here. Why do you have to drag Justin away and ruin it?" she demanded.

Regina blushed. She still felt woozy, and she really wanted to get outside. But now that looked impossible.

"Come over and sit down," Jan added in a sinister voice. She grinned at the others. "Don't you think Regina needs a little something to pep her up? She looks kind of pale."

"Speaking of pale," Buzz said, taking a small packet of white powder out of his bag, "would you all just take a look at this!"

The group in the circle was quiet for a minute, staring at the packet. Jan, Jay, and Molly all eyed it hungrily. Regina couldn't believe that Molly's little brother Ty was sitting in the circle too. Wasn't he way too young?

"Justin," she said uncertainly, "I really think I'd better be going."

Justin leaned closer to her. "Look," he said under his breath, "I don't want to leave Molly here as long as Buzz is around. I don't trust him. Cocaine is one thing—I know she can handle that. But he's been trying to get her to try heroin, and I'm afraid if I leave her, she might give in. I can't stand to see that happen to her."

Regina's mouth dropped open. "Heroin?" she repeated in amazement.

"Just sit down with us for half an hour. Then I promise I'll take you home," Justin pleaded.

Mesmerized, Regina followed Justin back to where the group was sitting around a coffee table. She didn't feel strong enough to walk home—her legs felt wobbly. Besides, she didn't really know the way from here. It couldn't hurt to wait for Justin, she decided, watching as Buzz took a razor blade out of his pocket and began to cut the powder into fine white lines on a large mirror.

"What's he doing?" she whispered to Justin.

Unfortunately the song they had been listening to stopped just before she spoke, and everyone in the circle heard her. Jan began to hoot with laughter. "Don't tell me you've never seen anyone do lines of coke before," she said scornfully.

Regina's eyes widened. "I haven't," she said truthfully.

"I bet you're too scared even to get near the stuff," Jay said, putting his arm around Jan's shoulder and looking at Regina with disgust.

Regina looked curiously at the white substance on the mirror. It looked like powdered sugar. So this was cocaine, she thought, her face still flushed from the effects of the beer she'd drunk. Funny . . . she would have expected it to look scarier somehow. She couldn't imagine that innocuous white powder really doing anything to anyone.

"What does it do to you?" she asked with interest.

Molly's eyes were huge as she watched Buzz. "Regina, you don't know what you're missing," she said in a dazed voice. "Coke is absolutely fantastic. You take one snort and all of a sudden nothing matters. You forget about school, about your family, about—" She glanced quickly at Justin and then away again. "About all your problems. You just feel terrific."

Regina blinked. "But can't it hurt you? Don't you get hooked on it?"

Buzz laughed. "Is that what they're teaching now? That you can get addicted to coke? Listen," he added, "if you've got the money, this stuff is the passport to heaven. It won't hurt you, it won't make you fat, it won't get you hooked, all it'll do is make you happy."

"Forget it," Jan said with disgust. "Don't waste any of it on her. She's only good for one thing . . . and that's stealing boyfriends."

Molly giggled—a high, taunting giggle that Regina could hardly bear.

A shocked silence fell on the group, and everyone looked at Regina, waiting to see what she'd do. Regina felt her cheeks burn. A feeling so strong she couldn't even name it welled up inside her. Suddenly she was sick of being "Miss Goody-Goody," of sitting quietly and listening to Jan's nasty comments. For once she felt like doing something completely out of character.

"I'd like to try it," she said. Everyone stared, and she felt a brief flash of triumph. There! she thought. So much for Nicholas and Bruce and her parents and Elizabeth and everyone else who thought Regina was good and quiet and calm and dependable. For once— just for once—she wanted to do something wild. Something that would shut Jan up and wipe that mean, stupid smirk off her face forever.

Buzz was explaining to her how to snort the cocaine. He showed her how to hold one nostril with her finger while she leaned forward over the line of white pow- der, a rolled up twenty-dollar bill used like a tube to sniff up the powder through the other nostril. It seemed perfectly simple . . . and all she had to do was sniff really hard.

"It'll burn a little at first, and then you'll feel an amazing rush," Buzz said, giving her a welcoming smile. Even Justin was grinning. Everyone seemed to think it was great that she was being such a good sport.

Regina leaned over the table and felt dizzy for a second. "Wow," she said, "I'm not used to drinking. Will it matter that I had a few beers first?"

"Nope," Molly promised her. "Go for it, Regina. You're about to have the time of your life!"

At first all Regina felt was a sudden sharp burning sensation in her nose. That was it. She felt exactly the way she had before she'd snorted the coke—only maybe a little less scared. Suddenly it seemed idiotic to have cared.

"Have her do another line," Molly said. "Sometimes you don't feel anything the first time."

"No way," Justin argued.

"Have her do another line," Molly said again. Her voice sounded like iron. Regina couldn't move. She just kept thinking how stupid she'd been to think this was a big deal.

"This is great!" Regina said, grinning happily as Jan led her back to the table and held her head down.

"Sniff up, baby. You need another hit," Jan said. "Buzz, help me."

The next thing Regina knew she saw her own face as she leaned back down over the mirror. A long line of white powder zoomed up beneath her. "Snort it," Jan commanded, pushing her face down toward the glass.

Regina tried to protest, but she couldn't. The next thing she knew the inside of her nose felt like fire, and her heart began to pound. "Wow," she said weakly, lifting up her head. "I guess . . . I guess I'm really kind of high."

Everyone laughed, and Regina laughed too. She felt so weird. She felt as if she could do absolutely anything—as if she were the most powerful person in the whole world. But something was wrong with her chest. Her heart was beating really fast, as if she'd been running. She couldn't really breathe.

"What's that noise?" she said thickly to Justin, reaching out weakly for his arm.

"What noise?" he demanded, still grinning at her.

"Beating," Regina said. "Like drums."

"Hey, I think she's going to be sick," Molly said, anxious. "Why is her face so pale?"

"Like drums," Regina repeated.

"Her pulse is really fast," Justin said, his hand on her wrist. "That must be what she means about drums. I think she's feeling her heartbeat."

"Get her to lie down. She'll be OK," Buzz said nonchalantly. He handed the rolled-up bill to Jan.

"I think I'm sick," Regina said, struggling for control. Her face was ashen now, and it was almost impossible to understand her. "My chest hurts," she added, putting her hand over her heart. "Is that supposed to happen?"

Justin turned to Molly and Jan with a frown. "Turn down the music," he ordered. "She needs to lie down for a second, that's all."

He picked Regina up in his arms then and carried her over to the couch. Her breathing was ragged and her face was ghostly pale. "Get some wet paper towels," Justin ordered Ty. He leaned over her, his own face blanching as he listened to her tortured breathing.

"Molly," he said a minute later, "call 911. I think she's passed out."

"Don't be an idiot!" Buzz hollered. "You're going to call the *cops*?"

"We've got to do something," Justin said grimly. "There's something wrong with her, Buzz. Look at the way she's breathing."

"Wait a minute. Someone's at the door," Ty squealed, running to answer it.

And everyone froze as the door burst open and two policemen raced into the room, with Nicholas Morrow right behind them.

Eleven

"What have you done to my sister?" Nicholas hollered, giving Justin a shove that sent him flying as he fought his way through the crowd around the couch where Regina was lying.

"O'Riley, call an ambulance. I'm going after that guy," Sergeant Henderson said grimly, grabbing his radio and spinning around in pursuit of Buzz, who was running in the direction of the back door. The rest of the group was frozen. Someone had pulled the plug on the stereo when the policemen burst in, and now a terrified silence prevailed as Nicholas bent down over Regina, who was tossing fitfully on the sofa, her face a ghastly shade of white.

"We don't know what happened," Justin said, looking terrified. "She . . . uh, she did two lines of cocaine, and the next thing we knew . . ."

Sergeant O'Riley radioed in to headquarters, holding the radio close to his mouth. "We need an ambulance here right away at Forty-five Los Brisos," he said rapidly. "Subject's name is Regina Morrow. We've got her brother with us, and we need to contact the parents as soon as possible."

"They're at the country club," Nicholas said.

"Gibson, call the country club and have the Morrows paged. Tell them it's an emergency and we'll meet them at the hospital." Sergeant O'Riley looked grim. "And tell the paramedics we need oxygen. She's having trouble breathing."

"O'Riley, check her pulse," Gibson's voice crackled through the radio.

The policeman hurried over to the couch and picked Regina's limp wrist up in his hand. "She's fast—very fast," he said into the radio. "I'm getting forty beats in fifteen seconds."

"Roger. We've got an ambulance on its way. Try to keep her still and loosen her clothing, and clear everyone out of the way so the paramedics can get to her," Gibson advised.

Molly burst into tears. "We didn't mean anything," she said, terrified. "Officer, is she going to be all right?"

Sergeant O'Riley frowned, still holding Regina's wrist in his hand. "I hope so," he said.

Just then Regina opened her eyes. "Nicholas," she said thickly, closing her lids again.

Nicholas dropped down beside her. "I'm right here, Regina," he whispered. "Tell me what you need."

With an effort she opened her eyes again. "Nicholas," she said again. It seemed to take every bit of energy she had to say his name. "Tell them . . . tell them . . ." she said dully, her head rolling from side to side. "It wasn't anyone's fault," she whispered hoarsely.

Nicholas put both hands on her shoulders. "I'm listening," he said again. "Don't talk if it hurts you, Regina. Are you OK?"

"You were always . . . you were always such a *good* brother," Regina said. Suddenly she struggled to sit up, her eyes trying to focus on Molly. "Liz . . . where's Liz?" she mumbled. "I want to see Liz . . . and Bruce. Nicholas, find them."

The effort of trying to move seemed to exhaust her, and the next minute Regina had passed out completely.

"The ambulance is here!" Justin cried. "Get out of the way so they can bring in the stretcher!"

Nicholas jumped up, his eyes flashing. "I need to use the phone," he said urgently. "Sergeant, I'll be just a second. I'm going to ride with her in the back of the ambulance." He practically knocked over a chair in his haste to get to the telephone, and he could feel himself tremble violently as he dialed Lila Fowler's number.

His sister had asked to see Elizabeth and Bruce, and Nicholas was going to do what he could to get them to the hospital to be waiting for her when she came to.

Mayhem broke out at the Fowlers' when Elizabeth hung up the phone and told the group that Regina

103

was being rushed to the hospital. Bruce went dead white, then grabbed his car keys. "Come on," he said to Elizabeth. "Let's go."

"Wait a minute," Jeffrey said, putting his arm around Elizabeth. "I want to come," he told her, tipping her face up and staring deep into her eyes. "I want to be there with you, Liz."

"Me too," Enid said. "Liz, let Jeffrey and me come. You may need us."

Elizabeth trembled. "Nicholas said she asked for Bruce and me," she told them. "He wants everyone else to stay put for now. I promise I'll call the minute I learn anything."

Jessica looked as if she were about to burst into tears. "Poor Regina! Do they think it's an overdose? What on earth did those horrible people do to her?"

"It's all my fault," Bruce said, his face contorted. "If I hadn't acted like such a jerk . . ."

Amy flinched. "You couldn't help it," she said pathetically, but no one looked at her.

"This isn't a question of fault," Elizabeth said. "Come on, Bruce. We want to be there so if she asks for us again—"

She barely even knew what she was saying. Nicholas said it was serious. He said to hurry, she kept thinking. What did that mean, "serious"? What happened to you if you had a bad reaction to cocaine? She couldn't even imagine Regina smoking a cigarette, let alone trying cocaine! Her heart pounded as she tried to think what the poor girl must be going through. It was so frightening, so incredibly frightening. . . .

"She's going to be all right," Elizabeth said, not sure if she meant what she was saying.

"Liz, I know it's my fault," Bruce said brokenly. Tears were coursing down his face, and Elizabeth felt her heart go out to him.

"Don't be crazy. It isn't your fault. You can't let yourself think that way or you'll go nuts," Elizabeth said. If anyone was to blame, it was *she*. She had handled everyone wrong from the start. If she'd told Regina the truth about Bruce and Amy sooner, the girl never would have been humiliated at their barbecue. She might not have been driven to join Justin and his crowd. And in any case, once she found out that there was supposed to be drugs at Molly's party, Elizabeth should have done *everything* in her power to keep Regina from going. Instead . . .

But it was insane to think this way. They just had to concentrate their efforts on praying that their friend would be all right.

"OK," Bruce said several minutes later, pulling his Porsche into a parking space in front of the Joshua Fowler Memorial Hospital. "Let's go."

Elizabeth felt her heartbeat quicken as she saw the ambulance in front of the emergency room entrance, its lights still flashing. Two squad cars were parked in front as well. She and Bruce hurried into the emergency room, and the first person they saw was Nicholas, whose haggard face told them the worst wasn't over.

"My parents are in there," he said, jerking his head toward a closed door at the back of the emergency room. "They're talking to a heart specialist named Dr. Leonard. It looks like Regina had a heart attack from the cocaine."

"Where is she?" Elizabeth demanded, grabbing Nicholas's arm for support.

"She's in a treatment room. They're trying as hard as they can to revive her," Nicholas said grimly. "I called you guys because she asked for you. The last time she spoke . . ." His eyes filled with tears, and he blinked hard. "I think she wanted to tell you it was OK. She wanted so badly to tell you both something."

Neither Bruce nor Elizabeth knew what to say. But they didn't have time to speak in any case. Dr. Leonard was emerging from his office with Mr. and Mrs. Morrow, who looked too dazed even to focus on the scene before them. Mrs. Morrow had been sobbing, and her beautiful face was as white as a sheet.

"Nicholas," Mr. Morrow said heavily, putting his arm around his son, "we're all going to have to be incredibly brave tonight—for your sister's sake. Dr. Leonard doesn't think she's going to make it."

It felt as if the walls were caving in on Elizabeth. At first she didn't think she'd heard him right. But from the look on Nicholas's face she realized there was no denying it.

Mr. Morrow thought Regina was going to die. But Elizabeth just couldn't believe it. Regina was young—

and strong. She could recover from a heart attack, couldn't she? She was in a good hospital with good doctors. Elizabeth knew they could save her.

They had to. That was all there was to it.

The two hours Elizabeth and Bruce spent in the emergency room with the Morrows were the longest Elizabeth could ever remember. She knew it would be impossible to describe the agony of waiting with Regina's parents and brother while the doctors did everything humanly possible to revive Regina. Just before midnight the Morrows were all ushered into Dr. Leonard's office, and Elizabeth knew it was over. She and Bruce stared at each other, too frightened to acknowledge what was happening.

"You two are friends of Regina's, aren't you?" a younger doctor said then, sitting down beside them and looking at them gravely. "I'm sorry. We tried everything, but there was no hope." He shook his head, wiping his exhausted eyes with one hand. "It's absolutely tragic," he whispered. "Such a waste. Such an incredible waste."

Bruce broke down completely then, sobs wracking his body. Elizabeth felt simply too numb to cry. She felt as if the wind had been knocked out of her.

"Doctor, what happened?" Bruce choked out. "Was it poisoned, the stuff she took? How could it kill her?"

"We don't know exactly what happened yet," the internist said wearily. "All we can say for sure right now is that Regina took a lethal amount of cocaine tonight and experienced an extremely rare reaction—rapid acceleration of the heartbeat, which brought on sudden cardiac failure. It's possible that a heart murmur she's had since birth may have contributed to this, but we won't know until—" He stopped short, seeing the looks on their faces. "I'm sorry," he said then, putting his arms around them both. "You're very young to lose someone you love."

The door to the emergency room swung open then and Nicholas burst in, his eyes swollen with tears. "Regina's dead," he said brokenly.

Elizabeth would never forget the look on his face as long as she lived.

"You've got to drink this," Jeffrey commanded, bringing Elizabeth a cup of steaming cocoa. "I'm not leaving until you do."

"Jeffrey, honey, I don't think she really feels like it right now," Mrs. Wakefield said gently.

Jeffrey, Enid, and Jessica had picked Elizabeth up from the hospital and brought her home, after having made sure Bruce was feeling strong enough to drive himself home. Now they were all sitting in the living room, staring at each other. No one knew what to say.

"I just keep thinking of her parents," Mr. Wakefield cried. "It's such a waste! She was such a bright, lovely girl. . . . She had her whole life in front of her!"

Enid put her hands over her ears. "I can't stand it," she said. "I keep thinking that in a minute someone's going to come in and say the whole thing is just a bad dream. But this is really happening."

"You've got to stop feeling responsible," Jeffrey said to Elizabeth. "I can tell from your face how much you're torturing yourself."

Elizabeth's eyes welled up with tears. "I can't even think," she said brokenly. "Every time I try to think, I see her face and wonder what it's going to be like to be at school and never see her again. . . ." She began to sob in earnest. "It was our fault," she said brokenly. "If we hadn't deserted her . . . if we'd been around for her—"

"Honey, you can't think that way. You're only torturing yourself—Jeffrey is right," Mr. Wakefield said gently. But it was of little use. Elizabeth was crying now as if she'd never stop.

It was impossible to believe Regina was gone forever. Elizabeth just couldn't accept it. Bad as blaming herself was, at least it took her mind—at least partially—off the horror of admitting her friend was really and truly dead.

Twelve

Sweet Valley High was like another world when
the twins arrived there on Monday morning.
Word had spread like wildfire, and by this point everyone knew the terrible news. Usually the hallways
were lively on Monday mornings, filled with students
catching up on the events of the weekend, but that
Monday all was silent and subdued. Students spoke
in muted voices, and no one smiled. Neither Justin
nor Molly was in school, and everyone stayed away
from Jan Brown and her friends. On the p.a. system
during the morning announcements, the principal,
Mr. Cooper, came on and said that there would be a
brief assembly at eleven o'clock. The twins were in
homeroom when the announcement was made, and
they glanced at each other meaningfully. No doubt
Mr. Cooper wanted to make a public announcement
to squelch gossip.

Elizabeth thought that was a good thing. As it was,
rumors were flying. She heard someone say Regina
had been killed by an overdose of speed. Someone else

said she'd been poisoned. Obviously the sooner an "official" statement came out, the better for everyone concerned.

But Elizabeth couldn't bring herself to believe that whatever Mr. Cooper had to say would really change her own feelings. Her guilt pangs were bad enough. But the real suffering came not from her own sense of responsibility, but her sorrow for Regina. However hard she tried, she simply could not imagine that Regina was really dead. She kept anguishing over the thought of Regina's laughing face . . . her enthusiasm for little things. The injustice was so dreadful that she could barely stand it. Why Regina? What had Regina ever done to deserve this kind of terrible end?

Accompanying her sense of sorrow was a feeling of pure rage unlike anything Elizabeth had ever experienced before. She knew it was wrong to blame anyone, but she couldn't help feeling that if Regina hadn't met Justin and his friends, none of this would have happened. Regina would still be alive.

In fact, Elizabeth was glad that neither Justin nor Molly had showed up at school. She didn't think she could control herself if she saw either one of them. And she knew she wasn't alone in her feelings. Bruce kept saying he wanted to kill Justin, and the rest of their friends seemed to feel exactly the same way. It might not make sense to feel so angry, but pure grief was too hard to bear. At least blaming Justin and the others helped by allowing them all to find a target for their rage.

"I think they should be locked up for the rest of their lives," Lila intoned as a subdued group wended its way toward the auditorium just before noon. "I can't stand them for what they did to Regina."

Jeffrey patted Lila consolingly on her shoulder. "Let's just wait and listen to what Mr. Cooper has to say. I'm sure the police are going to take *some* kind of action."

"Maybe that's why Justin and Molly aren't in school today," Jessica suggested. "Maybe they're already in prison!"

"I didn't know you could die from cocaine," Caroline Pearce said miserably. "My older sister has friends who claim it's great stuff!"

"Yeah, I'll bet," Winston said unhappily. "I know one thing—I'm never going to try it."

"Me neither," Lila seconded. "I know some of my dad's colleagues have kids who use coke all the time. Boy, I'm sure glad I never wanted to." She shuddered.

Elizabeth felt numb as she walked beside Jeffrey and Enid into the auditorium. She wished there was some way *Regina* could have known in advance how dangerous the drug was. It seemed terrible that they were all finding out now—only because Regina had become a victim.

Mr. Cooper called the school to attention and cleared his throat. Usually students made jokes when they saw the bald principal, calling him "Chrome Dome" or horsing around. But today there was silence as he stood behind the podium to address them.

112

"I'm going to be very brief," he said quietly. "As some of you may already have heard, something awful occurred over the weekend. Regina Morrow died of cardiac failure following the use of cocaine on Saturday night."

Silence greeted this announcement. No one knew what to say or do next.

"Now I know you're all stunned and horrified by this news," Mr. Cooper continued. "Some of you may want to call the Morrows and offer your condolences. They have asked me to ask you to leave them in peace for the time being. Understandably they are all deeply shocked and need time—as we will all need time—to adjust to this tragic event." He cleared his throat. "They told me anyone who wishes to, may send condolence contributions to the drug rehabilitation program at Fowler Memorial Hospital. Their fervent hope is that by educating other people, senseless deaths— like Regina's—may be avoided."

Scattered applause followed this, and Mr. Cooper cleared his throat again. "The Morrows have asked me to tell you two things today. First, a memorial service will be held in this auditorium on Friday after school. You are all welcome to attend. Nicholas, Regina's older brother, has agreed to come on behalf of the family and say a few words of tribute. The funeral, of course, will be for family members only." He looked meaningfully out at the audience.

"They also asked me to explain the facts of the incident as far as we understand them to date, so that no one need be confused and there need be no rumors about the cause of her death. Regina died of a rare form of heart complication caused by an accelerated heartbeat. This, in turn, was caused by a sudden intake of cocaine which was too great for her system to bear." He paused for a moment. "The police are still investigating the whereabouts of the man believed to have supplied Regina with the drug, and obviously any information any of you have on him should be reported at once. The Morrows asked me explicitly to tell you that no one else is being held responsible for Regina's death. The police are making some decisions in individual cases about use and possession of drugs, but that's it." He looked meaningfully out at the assembly. "In no instance is anyone to be treated as if he or she had any responsibility in Regina's death. That's all. I'll see you all Friday afternoon."

Elizabeth felt her cheeks burn as she got up from her seat. She didn't care what the Morrows said about this. She couldn't help blaming Molly. It was *her* party, wasn't it? *She* was the one who had let Buzz come. And no doubt she was the one who encouraged Regina to try cocaine in the first place.

Whatever the Morrows said, Molly was at least partly to blame. And how was Elizabeth supposed to hide her feelings when the girl finally came back to school?

"Liz!" Jessica cried, hurrying into the house with an envelope in her hand. It was Tuesday afternoon, and Elizabeth was chopping onions for the casserole she was making for dinner. "Look—it's a letter for you. From Regina."

Elizabeth dropped the knife, her eyes widening with disbelief. "What are you talking about?" she demanded.

"The return address says 'Regina Morrow'." Jessica thrust the letter into her sister's hands. "Open it, Liz." From Jessica's wide-eyed expression Elizabeth could tell that Jessica felt as baffled as she did, looking at the envelope. It was as if none of it had really happened. As if Regina were still perfectly OK and the whole nightmare had never happened.

Elizabeth got up from the table, turning the letter over and over in her hands. "I will. But I'd like to read it alone," she said softly. And ignoring the look of hurt on her twin's face, she took the letter upstairs.

"Dear Liz," the letter began.

I have a feeling this is going to sound a little bit stilted—forgive me, but I'm in a hurry (Justin is about to pick me up to go over to Molly's), and besides, what I have to say is hard to admit. I owe you an apology. You've been a good friend to me all along. I was furious with you for concealing what happened with Bruce and Amy from me. The truth is, *I* did a lot of concealing myself. I never admitted to myself that Bruce and I had drifted apart. He isn't to blame either. Sometimes couples just change and grow apart. Seeing how jealous Molly has been has helped me to see that Amy wasn't really to blame at all. No one can really break up a couple in love.

I owe you an apology because I see now that you tried to act in my best interest. I've always admired you so much, Liz. You were just trying to protect me, and I blew the whole thing out of proportion.

As far as warning me about Justin and Molly . . . well, I guess if I were really secure, I wouldn't have to act so defensive. Maybe next time I'll be a little more willing to listen to you. You've always proved right in the past—I don't see why I should stop listening now!

Your friend,
Regina

P.S.—I hope you didn't think it's strange that I've said all this in a letter, but somehow it's too hard to say on the phone. I really am sorry, and hope our friendship will last forever.

R.M.

Elizabeth read the letter several times, her eyes filling with tears. All at once she felt a number of conflicting feelings. On the one hand she felt tremendously relieved, knowing Regina had forgiven her before her death. She also felt such nostalgic sorrow at the familiar tone of the letter. It was as if Regina were right there in the room with her. "I really am sorry, and hope our friendship will last forever," she read aloud.

The tears spilled over then. The irony of that simple sentence hit her really hard—just thinking how hopeful Regina must have felt when she wrote those words. Because the truth was that things just didn't last forever. Not friendship, not human lives. Elizabeth knew this before, but she had never felt it.

This was the first time someone she truly loved had died. And the kind of loneliness she felt right then was so profound, she didn't think it would ever go away.

The tension in the auditorium on Friday afternoon was almost unbearable. For days no one had talked of anything but Regina's memorial service. Nicholas had chosen Elizabeth to make a presentation, and her palms were sweating as she waited in the wings along with Enid and Jeffrey. She wanted so badly to say something that would be true to Regina's memory. She had written draft after draft of a short speech, but nothing seemed right. In the end she had decided just to speak from her heart. Something told her Regina would have preferred it that way anyway.

The auditorium lights were dimmed as the service got under way. First the choir sang a chorus from a German mass which Regina had always loved. Candles were lit during the singing, and the entire school listened with awe.

Then Mr. Collins got up to speak. He had been Regina's favorite teacher and was loved and respected by everyone. Elizabeth listened eagerly as he began to talk about Regina. Somehow she felt she could derive strength from what he said.

"Many of us in this room today were lucky enough to know Regina Morrow," he said in a loud, strong voice. "Some of us were lucky enough to be her friend. A few—a very few—were lucky enough to have loved her and to have been loved by her in return. But I think we all share this afternoon in a profound feeling of loss. It is occasionally claimed that young people have no understanding of suffering—that they are exempt from tragedy. Your loss this past week shows how false such a claim is. The truth is, no one is exempt from tragedy. To be human is to be susceptible to pain."

Silence followed as Mr. Collins cleared his throat. "My job here at Sweet Valley High is to teach English literature. I suppose if literature has a lesson for us, it is how to learn from the lessons life teaches us— how to endure. I cannot possibly comfort any one of you as you grieve for Regina. Nor can I offer solace to her brother Nicholas, who has come here today in her behalf—or her parents, who are at home suffering their loss in their own way. What I can say is that I know each and every one of us will remember Regina Morrow. She was a brave, delightful, beautiful girl whose life was a model for many of us. Her courage and her perseverance taught me a great deal, as I'm sure it did you."

This last remark was followed by another silence. "If there is anything we can learn from this tragedy, let us learn it," Mr. Collins added. "For Regina to have died in vain would be unthinkable. We must all do what we can to make sure this kind of senseless tragedy never happens again."

A brief silence followed. It was Elizabeth's turn now to speak, and she took a deep breath, stepping out onto the stage and facing her classmates. Suddenly she knew exactly what she wanted to say.

"I thought about bringing a prepared speech to read to you about Regina," she began in a clear, natural voice. "But somehow each time I tried to write something, it seemed wrong to me. Regina would've hated something like that. Everything about Regina was natural, spontaneous, and unpretentious. The things she loved—like spending time with close friends, reading, taking long walks by the beach—were simple things." Elizabeth's eyes filled briefly with tears, but she blinked them back. She had to be strong—for Regina's sake.

"I don't really feel there's anything I can say about Regina's death, which is too tragic and too terrible for me to fathom," she continued. "What I can say something about is Regina's *life*. I never knew anyone who faced problems—tough problems—with as much courage and humor. I never knew anyone who so gracefully managed to combine strength and gentleness. Regina was a fine person and a wonderful friend, and I know I'll never ever forget her."

"That was wonderful," Jeffrey said, putting his arm around her as she stumbled off stage, her eyes blinded with tears.

Elizabeth hugged him gratefully. She knew she had spoken her heart, and it helped somehow to feel she'd been able to express her feelings in a way she thought Regina might have liked.

Nicholas was the last to speak. He was wearing a dark suit, and he looked pale and exhausted, but his voice was clear and strong as he spoke, and his hands were steady as he picked up a piece of paper. "I have a poem I want to read this afternoon by a poet Regina loved named Edna St. Vincent Millay," he told them. "But before I read the poem I want to say something to all of you. The months Regina spent in this school were the happiest of her life, and the friendships she formed with you mattered to her more than anything else in the world. Nothing can give Regina back to us. All I can beg of you is to learn from her tragic example how fleeting life is. There are two things we all have to do: First, we all have to do everything in our power to protect ourselves and our friends from danger. And second, we have to live every moment as fully as we can. Regina tried to live that way, and the only consolation in her loss is knowing the joy she experienced in her short life."

He cleared his throat, then picked up the sheet of paper and began to read as the auditorium listened in awe. " 'Dirge Without Music,' " he read.

"I am not resigned to the shutting away of loving hearts in the hard ground.
So it is, and so it will be, for so it has been, time

out of mind;
Into the darkness they go, the wise and the lovely; crowned
With lilies and laurels they go; but I am not resigned.

"Lovers and thinkers, into the earth with you.
Be one with the dull, the indiscriminate dust.
A fragment of what you felt, of what you knew,
A formula, a phrase remains—but the best is lost.

"The answers quick and keen, the honest look, the laughter, the love—
They are gone. They are gone to feed the roses.
Elegant and curled
Is the blossom. Fragrant is the blossom. I know.
But I do not approve.
More precious was the light in your eyes than all the roses in the world.

"Down, down, down into the darkness of the grave
Gently they go, the beautiful, the tender, the kind;
Quietly they go, the intelligent, the witty, the brave.
I know. But I do not approve. And I am not resigned."

In a kind of daze, Elizabeth, Enid, and Jeffrey got up from their seats offstage. Quietly the crowd made its way toward the two doors in the back of the room.

"That was beautiful, Nicholas," Elizabeth said, putting her arm around him.

"Thanks," Nicholas said, clearing his throat with an effort.

But he wasn't looking at her. He was staring at the back of the auditorium, where Justin Belson was getting up from his seat.

It was the first time Justin had appeared at school that week. Elizabeth couldn't get over the change in him. His face looked haggard, and she was sure he hadn't slept in days. But that wasn't the only difference. His eyes looked haunted, and his expression was grief-stricken. Her heart went out to him as she watched him move slowly toward the door.

But Elizabeth wasn't the only one watching Justin just then. On the other side of the auditorium Molly Hecht was sitting by herself, watching Justin leave. She wanted so badly to speak to him. They hadn't talked once since the whole tragedy had taken place.

Screwing up her courage, Molly crossed the room and put her hand on Justin's shoulder. "Justin," she said in a low voice.

He looked down at her in silence, pulling away from her touch.

"Please," she said urgently. "Justin, we need to talk."

But Justin wouldn't listen to her. He jerked away as if her touch had burned him, and without a backward glance he turned and hurried away from her down the crowded corridor.